Cathy Bramley is a British ████████ romance novels, and ha ████████ million copies worldwid█ ████ ████ ██ave hit the UK bestseller list and have been nominated for several awards, including the British Book of the Year 2023.

Also by Cathy Bramley

A Merry Little Christmas
The Sunrise Sisterhood
Merrily Ever After
The Summer That Changed Us
The Merry Christmas Project
My Kind of Happy
A Patchwork Family
A Vintage Summer
A Match Made in Devon
Hetty's Farmhouse Bakery
The Lemon Tree Café
White Lies and Wishes
Comfort and Joy
The Plumberry School of Comfort Food
Wickham Hall
Appleby Farm
Conditional Love
Ivy Lane

The Surprise Visitor

A QUICK READS ORIGINAL

Cathy Bramley

ORION

Chapter One

Jo Potter finished arranging the bouquet of flowers which had been delivered earlier and stood back to admire them. They were gorgeous: roses, lilies, tulips, all competing for attention among frothy leaves. It had been her favourite task of the day so far. She'd had so much practice doing huge displays for the church, when she'd been the vicar's wife, that she could do it with her eyes closed.

Her other jobs this morning had been nowhere near as glamorous: she had washed floors, scrubbed toilets and vacuumed enough cat hair from the sofas to stuff a cushion. Fergus the long-haired tabby cat was adorable, but quite how one small animal could make such a mess was a mystery.

Cleaning a big old Victorian house was hard work, but at least it kept her fit. She was stronger now at forty-one than at any time in her life. She was almost finished for the day now, thank goodness. She was exhausted, not to mention very hot and sweaty.

Her previous house, a vicarage, had been a similar size to this one, next to the church where her ex-husband, Duncan, had been the vicar. Their home had been the heart of the church community, and she had loved it. Although she hadn't had an official role, she'd been involved in everything from fundraising to hosting Christmas lunch for the elderly. Wonderful years full of happy memories until one day, her world had come crashing down and life had changed forever.

Still, it was best not to think about the past. No one knew her in her new town of Boddington and she kept herself to herself. She had learnt the hard way that in a place where everyone knew your business, there was nowhere to hide when things went wrong. Now she rented a tiny, terraced house, with a kitchen so narrow that when she and her daughter Faith were both in it, they had to walk sideways like crabs to get past each other.

The last couple of years had been tough, but Jo had a lot to be grateful for: she was healthy, she had this part-time job, and Faith. And then there was her best friend Eve, who she'd known for decades. That was more than a lot of people had.

She put the kettle on to make herself a drink before she left. There was a shiny chrome coffee machine sitting in pride of place beside the kettle, but Jo opened the jar of instant as usual.

The kettle came to the boil and clicked off just as her boss, Maria, walked in wearing a tight leopard print top and leather skirt. If Duncan were here, he'd mutter under his breath about Maria's outfit being disgraceful. When they were married, Jo had become used to dressing in a way that met with her husband's approval: necklines which didn't show cleavage and skirts always below the knee. He'd be horrified by Jo's scruffy cleaning uniform: old t-shirts she didn't mind splashing bleach on, and jeans that were baggy around her knees and bum.

Mind you, she really should stop thinking about what Duncan would say. She had nothing to do with him anymore.

'Coffee time?' Maria teased, wagging a finger at Jo. Her nails were perfectly shaped and painted a deep red. In contrast, Jo's were in shreds and the skin around them red and sore. There was no point wearing nail polish in this job, it would chip off straight away. 'Caught you having a little breather, have I?'

Jo hid a sigh. It was typical of her boss to notice that the kettle was switched on but be completely oblivious to the sparkling counter-tops and gleaming taps. 'Just a quick one before I leave, I'm parched. Do you want one?'

'No time, the taxi is on its way,' Maria said. 'I'm so lucky to have a husband who spoils me.'

'You are,' said Jo, trying not to sound envious.

It was Maria's birthday, and she was going to London to meet her husband, Nigel, who was already there on business. He was taking her to see *Moulin Rouge* in the West End. Jo had always wanted to see that show, but Duncan had taken one look at the revealing costumes and forbidden it.

'It's so kind of you to look after Fergus while I'm away,' said Maria.

'No bother at all, I haven't got any plans.' Jo tried not to compare Maria's evening with hers. She would be on her own, as Faith was staying with her boyfriend, Brad. She would probably just eat toast and watch old episodes of *Friends*.

There was a toot of a car horn outside.

'There's my taxi,' Maria said, with a squeak of excitement. 'You'll lock up properly, won't you?'

'Don't worry, you can trust me,' said Jo.

'I know I can.' Maria held eye contact, making Jo blush. 'And if you really don't have any plans while I'm away, perhaps you could do a bit of extra cleaning for me? The ovens are quite mucky.'

Jo's heart sank. She had always called professionals in to do the ovens in her own home – it was a job she detested. She swallowed the lump in her throat and tried to think about the extra money, and not about how times had changed. 'Of course, happy to help.'

Maria shimmied down the hall in her heels, picked up her suitcase and checked her reflection in the hall mirror. 'Oh Jo,' she said, as she opened the front door. 'There's a tiny smudge on the glass, just in the corner, can you . . . ?'

'Sure. Leave it with me,' said Jo flatly. Typical. The only comment Maria made about the cleaning was to point out something that she'd missed.

As soon as the door closed behind Maria, Jo carried the vase of flowers to the hall table. Then, removing her phone from her pocket, she took a photograph of the arrangement and sent it to her best friend, Eve, with a message.

Look at these beautiful blooms, and it's not even my birthday!

It wasn't really a lie, she reasoned, just not quite the truth. Compared with some of the whopping great fibs which Jo had told Eve over the past couple of years, it was pretty insignificant. If Eve ever found out about those... Jo shuddered; it was too awful to even consider. It must never, ever happen.

Chapter Two

Two minutes later, Jo was sitting down, enjoying her coffee when her mobile phone rang. She read the name of the caller on the screen and smiled. This person was always guaranteed to cheer her up.

'Eve!' Jo said. 'Hello! Lovely to hear from you.'

'I was going to text back to say how jealous I am of your flowers, and of having a husband who's still romantic after all those years of marriage.' Eve launched into the conversation without saying hello. 'But then— oh, hold on a second.'

'No worries.' Jo sipped her coffee while Eve spoke to somebody else in the background.

'Sorry about that. I'm on a train and had to show my ticket,' Eve continued. 'As I was saying, I thought why not give you a call instead, if you're free to chat? I know how busy you are with all your vicar's wife duties.'

Jo felt a pang of guilt; she didn't have any such duties these days, she wasn't even a wife anymore. But she forced a smile into her voice. 'Your timing is perfect, I'm having a moment's peace in the conservatory, looking out at the flower beds.'

'Sounds idyllic,' Eve sighed. 'I bet it's beautiful. I'd love to visit the new house one day. Not that it's new anymore.'

'Oh yes, you must.' Jo's heart squeezed with nerves. 'We'll have to sort out a date.'

'You keep saying that, but you've been there two years,' Eve grumbled. 'It's a good job I love you, otherwise I'd get a complex that you're avoiding me.'

'I'm not!' Thank goodness they weren't doing a video call; Jo could feel her face had gone red. 'It's busy now in the run-up to Easter, and then of course, wedding season starts, and the vicarage is bombarded with nervous brides and mothers.'

'Ugh,' said Eve. 'I don't envy you that.'

'It wasn't so bad,' Jo replied wistfully. 'Being a part of someone's big day was a privilege. And seeing young couples so in love, and excited about their future, used to make me believe in love again too.'

'Used to?' Eve pointed out. 'Don't you feel that way anymore?'

Whoops. Too late, Jo realised that she'd spoken in the past tense. 'Yes, yes, of course, I just meant that ... you know,' she stuttered. 'Wedding season ends, and you go back to the normal stuff, like funerals and visiting the sick in hospital.'

'Oh, right.' Eve seemed to accept her rambling explanation. 'Talking of the sick, how is Duncan now? Is he over his illness?'

'Umm.' Jo wracked her brains, trying to remember exactly what she'd said was wrong with him last time they had spoken. 'He's much better thanks.'

'It was a shame he missed your parents' anniversary party.'

Oh yes, Jo remembered now. She had sent Eve a few photos from the day. Eve had asked why Duncan wasn't in any of them and Jo had had to make up an excuse. She'd probably said he had a stomach bug.

'It was. But on the plus side, it made him a little bit slimmer, and he can do up his favourite trousers again.'

'He lost weight from having a headache?' Eve sounded confused. 'That's unusual.'

Damn. Jo had forgotten she'd told Eve that.

'He lost his appetite for a while, missed a few meals,' Jo blustered. 'Annoying how men can lose weight without putting much effort in.'

'Right.' Eve paused. 'But the main thing is, he's recovered.'

'Oh yes, back to his parishioners. You know how he is: busy, busy, busy.' Jo was at it again. Spinning more lies. In truth, she hadn't got a clue what Duncan was doing. Since the divorce was finalised, there was no need for her to be in contact with him. She preferred to put that part of her life in the past.

'Do you know,' said Eve, 'that it's twenty-five years since you and I first met. I was having a sort-out and found some old photos last weekend.'

'Gosh, really? I suppose it must be,' Jo marvelled. 'It was the first week of college when we were both sixteen.'

'And now look at us. In our forties and still friends.'

'Still *best* friends,' Jo said.

'Exactly! Which makes it even more crazy that it's been so long since I saw you,' said Eve. 'I miss you.'

'Me too.' Jo swallowed a lump in her throat.

'We really must . . .' both women said at the same time and laughed.

Jo thought about how much the two of them had been through together over the years, how much she'd love to see Eve again. But it would be a bit tricky now after everything that had happened in her own life. How she longed to tell

Eve the truth. She should have just been honest with her from the start. But her silly pride had got in the way and the longer she had left it, the harder it had become. Now she had lost track of all the lies she had told her oldest friend. She felt terribly ashamed, but didn't know what to do about it.

'I could come and see you?' Jo blurted out. 'Perhaps next weekend before it gets too busy here? Duncan can manage without me for a couple of days.'

There was such a long gap before Eve spoke that Jo thought the line had gone dead.

'Ordinarily, I'd love you to come to stay. But, er...' Eve cleared her throat. 'I've been meaning to tell you, I'm in the process of moving house. So it's not very convenient at the moment.'

Jo gasped. 'Oh my word! That is very big news indeed! I thought you loved your flat.'

'I do, but the flat is quite small and I've always wanted some outside space, so I've bought a cottage. Nowhere near as big as your place, but it's quite cute and it has a pretty little garden.'

'Eve! This is so exciting! Is it online? Send me a link, I'd love to see it.' Jo was thrilled for her, but couldn't help feeling hurt that such a major thing was happening in her best friend's life and this was the first she'd heard about it.

'It was all very spur of the moment. It isn't online, because I put an offer in before it was officially up for sale. I've got some pictures somewhere; I'll send you those.'

'That would be nice, please do.' Jo attempted to keep her voice light, but this all felt very peculiar. She didn't want to appear rude, but how could Eve afford to buy a house all of a sudden? For as long as she'd known Eve, she had never had very much money.

'Gosh, is that the time? I'd better go,' said Eve abruptly. 'I promised myself I'd do some work on the train; I haven't done a thing yet and I've got a looming deadline.'

'But you're a driving instructor, what can you do on a train? What sort of deadline?'

'There's loads of paperwork in my job, you'd be amazed,' Eve replied with a high-pitched laugh. 'All very boring. I'd much rather be organising the church fundraising coffee mornings, or flower arranging like you. Still, it needs doing and I've got a long journey, so it's a perfect opportunity.'

'Oh, I see,' said Jo. 'Where are you going, anywhere nice?'

'Pardon?' Eve asked. 'Sorry, I think I've lost the signal. Hello?'

'I can hear you clearly,' said Jo.

'Hello? Hello? Oh dear, I think she's gone,' Eve muttered.

'No, I haven't, I'm—'

The line went dead and when Jo called her back all she got was Eve's voicemail. How very odd.

Chapter Three

Jo's name flashed up on Eve Langton's screen again. Eve switched the phone to silent. She felt awful for ignoring it, but even worse for telling lies. The line had been perfectly fine. Eve had been able to hear every word Jo was saying, but she'd had to end the call when she'd realised what a pickle she was getting into. She was so cross with herself for blurting out about her house move like that.

Her phone continued to vibrate; Eve imagined Jo at home wondering why she wasn't picking up. The other passengers on the train around her were probably thinking the same thing. She had chosen a window seat at a table for four passengers so she could work. Luckily, the girl opposite her wearing headphones seemed to be asleep and the other two seats were empty. She shoved her phone into her handbag and prayed that Jo would give up once the call had gone to voicemail a couple of times.

She'd been trying to work out a way to tell

Jo she was buying a new house for ages. And now she'd announced the news without preparing herself for the inevitable questions. Like for example, where on earth had the money come from to buy a house? And not just any old house. Eve had bought a thatched cottage in an expensive area in the Cotswolds. It had beamed ceilings, its own orchard and a little stream at the bottom of the garden. It was quite possibly the most beautiful house she had ever set eyes on.

Eve needed to come up with a good explanation as to how she was able to afford her dream house before the next time they spoke. There was no way in this world that she could admit to Jo the changes which had taken place in her life over the last couple of years. There was a risk that it would end their friendship, and Eve couldn't bear that. The more time that passed, the bigger and more frequent her lies were getting, so that nowadays conversations with Jo were filled with worry that she would slip up and catch herself out. Take for example, the real work she had to do on the train today. Jo would be stunned if she knew what Eve was doing. Of course there was some admin involved in being a driving instructor, but very rarely any deadlines. But the truth was that she hadn't taught anyone to drive for two years, not since her other career took off. Her exciting, successful new career which was earning her decent money for the first time in her life.

Talking of work, Eve really should get on. She lifted her bag onto the empty seat beside her, took out her new laptop and set it on the table. It had cost her a lot of money, but it was an investment, and she couldn't do her job without a fast machine and a comfortable keyboard.

An elderly man walked down the carriage and stood at the empty seat beside Eve. 'Is this anyone's seat?'

'No, please sit down,' said Eve, moving her bag onto the table.

'Nice bag,' said the girl, waking up and spotting the Mulberry logo on Eve's handbag.

'Thanks.' Eve gave an embarrassed smile. It had been a present to herself for a landmark achievement and was the first ever luxury item she'd ever owned.

'Where are we all off to, then?' the old man asked.

'I'm visiting a printer in Suffolk,' Eve told him. She moved her fingertip across the touchpad on her laptop to bring it to life, ready to begin.

'Interesting.' He nodded, folding his hands

across his stomach. 'In the printing business, are you?'

'Sort of,' said Eve. She felt rude giving him such a brief reply, but she really did have to do some work. She opened up the document she was working on and read through the paragraphs that she'd written yesterday.

'I'm going back to uni,' said the girl. She pulled a book out of her bag, lifting it up in front of her face to discourage further conversation.

Eve stared at the girl's book in joyous disbelief.

The cover had a picture of a woman in a dark cloak going up a stone staircase. It was a romance novel about a famous actress who had a steamy love affair with the presenter of a late-night radio show. It was called *The Midnight Secret Date* and it was written by Evelyn Lace.

But Evelyn Lace wasn't the author's real name. Eve knew this because the author's real name was Eve Langton. Her.

And the girl on the train opposite was reading her book. This was the moment Eve had dreamt of. Ever since her first book had been published, Eve had been dying to spot someone reading one of her novels in public. She knew she'd sold loads of books – she'd seen the numbers. But this, seeing someone in real life enjoying an Evelyn Lace book, meant more to her than anything. Would it be weird to get her phone out and take a picture of the girl reading it? Probably. Definitely. Eve forced herself to act cool.

Eve imagined herself tapping the girl on the shoulder and saying, 'I wrote that, I am Evelyn Lace.' But she couldn't do it, it would be embarrassing, and the girl would probably be too nervous to carry on reading it knowing she was being watched.

Eve turned to her laptop with renewed enthusiasm. Writing books was the hardest thing she had ever done, but she received messages every day from readers who told her how much they loved her stories. And now she'd actually seen it for herself. By the time she got off the train in Suffolk, she was sure she'd have written a whole chapter.

For the next thirty minutes, Eve concentrated on her writing. The old man dropped off to sleep, snoring lightly, and the girl remained glued to her book.

The train pulled into a station with a squeal of brakes. The train manager made an announcement about a short platform, and passengers charged past to disembark safely. Eve allow herself a break and glanced at her phone. There was a text message from Jo on the screen.

Couldn't get hold of you. Send pics of the
new house I need ALL the info! xxx

She was about to type a response when a middle-
aged woman appeared beside their table and
cleared her throat, pointing to the last spare seat
at their table on which the old man had put his
coat.

'Is this space taken?' she said loudly enough
to wake him.

'What?' The old man's eyes sprung open,
startled. 'No, allow me to move my coat, my
apologies.'

He stood, picked up his coat and waited in the
aisle while the new passenger took off hers. She
folded it meticulously and stowed it in the overhead storage rack. The old man then proceeded
to put his coat up there too.

'Not on top of mine!' the woman chided.

'I do beg your pardon,' said the old man,
adjusting his coat.

'No way! OMG!' The girl's mouth dropped
open, and she lowered the book to her chest.

'I'm sorry, but it's pure wool,' the woman protested. 'I don't want it creased like an old rag by
the time we arrive in Suffolk.'

Eve's heart leapt with pleasure. She knew
which bit the girl must have read, and that was

exactly the reaction she'd been hoping for. 'I think the young lady is referring to her book, not your coat.'

'Oh,' said the woman, curtly. 'Well, there's no need to shout.'

The girl nodded at Eve. 'It is so good. Can't put it down.'

Eve could have burst with joy. There was no finer compliment than that.

The old man squinted at the book to read the title. '*The Midnight Secret Date*. Not heard of that one. Would you recommend it?'

'Um.' The girl bit her lip, as if thinking what to say. 'Well, I like it.'

'Smut,' said the new woman, her mouth scrunched up in distaste.

'What do you mean?' said the old man.

'That book,' the woman nodded at it. 'Pure smut.'

Out of the corner of her eye, Eve noticed someone lift up their phone on the other side of the aisle. Probably taking a selfie, Eve decided and thought no more about it. She was more interested in the conversation between the passengers on her own table.

'It's a spicy romance, that's all.' The girl looked uncomfortable. 'Nothing wrong with that.'

'Spicy?' The old man looked confused.

'Full of sex,' said the woman and folded her arms. Pink spots had bloomed on her cheeks.

That was true. Eve's books were full of sex scenes. They had felt a bit awkward to write to begin with, but information from her publisher showed that the hotter the better when it came to romance books. This particular book had hit the bestseller list and had been translated into several languages across the world, so her publisher had been right.

Lots of people had read Evelyn Lace's books, but very few had met her in real life. She didn't do reader events, and if she had to have her photo taken, she dressed all in black, wore dark glasses and bright red lipstick. The world of publishing had been rife with rumours about who the mysterious Evelyn Lace could be, but so far she had managed to stay anonymous. Given this woman's attitude, Eve was quite glad nobody knew who she was.

'Oh I say.' The old man's eyes widened.

'There's nothing wrong with reading what you enjoy,' said Eve.

'Why books like these are so popular is a mystery,' said the woman. 'The writing is awful and the main characters lurch from one bed to another. Disgusting.'

Eve's jaw fell open. She was aware that her

books weren't everyone's cup of tea, and that was fine. But 'awful'? That was a bit mean.

'You should be ashamed of yourself.' The woman looked down her nose at the girl. 'Reading a book like that in public. There could be children present.'

The girl looked at the cover of the book very deliberately. 'Unless children have X-ray vision and can read the pages through the cover, where's the problem?'

'How do you know what it's about, if you haven't read it?' Eve asked her.

The woman straightened her spine. 'I'm very aware of what is going on in the world of books, and books by Evelyn Lace are trash.'

'Over a million readers might beg to differ,' Eve pointed out. 'Including me.'

The girl regarded her in surprise. 'You've read the *Secret Date* books?'

'Several times,' said Eve. Which was true. No need to admit that she'd *written* them too.

'Decent people read proper books,' said the woman with a sniff.

'I'm afraid I can't—' Eve began.

'What's this if it's not a proper book?' The girl waggled the paperback in front of the older woman crossly. 'A stone tablet? I read for pleasure and this book gives me that. I can read whatever I want, and I don't need anyone else's permission.'

Eve couldn't sit by and listen any longer, it wasn't fair. As the author, she should be the one to stand up for the book, not the reader. But before she could speak, she was interrupted by an announcement from the speaker above her head.

'Quick update here from your train manager. There's been an incident on the rail network. Our train is being held here while we await instructions. My apologies. Thank you for your patience.'

Damn. Eve glanced at the time. They were running half an hour late already. She was supposed to have lunch before watching the first copies of her new book *Summer Secret Date* come off the printing press. At this rate she would arrive too late, and they'd have started printing without her. The whole point of her visit was to film the very first books coming off the production line for social media and give the first ten copies away to her readers.

Her phone rang again. This time it was her publicist Gemma, and she answered straight away.

'How's it going?' Gemma asked.

'Slowly.' Eve explained about the delay.

'Oh no, total nightmare!' The publicist exclaimed. 'Poor you!'

'I'm sure it'll be fine; I can always skip lunch and go straight to the factory.'

'Thank you for being flexible.' Gemma breathed a sigh of relief. 'I'll let them know. Keep me posted.'

Eve promised that she would and ended the call.

The poor girl opposite was still having to defend Eve's book. 'I'm very grateful to the author for writing this book and so are my friends; Evelyn has given us sexual confidence to—'

'Good grief. Enough.' The woman held a hand up in front of her. 'I'm not sitting here listening to this.'

'I'm not enjoying listening to this either,' Eve said boldly, ready to side with the girl.

'You see!' said the woman, pointing at Eve as she stood up. 'She agrees. People who write this sort of thing are filthy as far as I'm concerned, and the readers are no better. I could not be friends with anyone who reads or writes this disgusting drivel. I don't want to be seen sitting by someone reading a book like that, so I'm moving seats. Goodbye.'

The woman whisked her coat down from the

overhead luggage rack and strutted away down the length of the carriage and into the next.

Filthy? Was that really how some people viewed spicy romance authors? Eve was so shocked that she couldn't speak.

There was a whistle of disbelief from the other side of the aisle. Eve saw the same person holding their phone up again. What was it with people taking selfies all the time?

'You're not filthy,' Eve told the girl. 'And neither is the author.'

Having said that, Eve was quite grateful that the woman hadn't known who she really was.

'Thanks,' the girl replied. 'No one has the right to tell another person what they should or shouldn't read.'

'Gosh, after all that drama, I need to find the loo.' The old man stood up. 'Excuse me, ladies.'

'This train delay is a nightmare,' said Eve, once he'd gone. She checked her watch. 'Where even are we?' She had been so wrapped up in her writing that she hadn't been paying attention.

'Boddington apparently,' said the girl.

'Oh?' Eve looked out of the window 'That's where my best friend lives.'

'You can go and visit her instead of the printers,' said the girl. 'That sounds way more fun.'

'Maybe.' Eve wrinkled her nose. In theory it

should be, but she would have to do some serious thinking before visiting Jo. Jo was going to have lots of questions, and Eve needed to work out how to answer them.

The girl went back to reading her book, her eyes skating eagerly across the pages. The temptation to talk to her about it was huge.

'By the way,' said Eve. 'I thought you defended yourself really well back then. And as you're obviously a big fan, I can arrange for you to get an early signed copy of Evelyn Lace's next book, if you like?'

'Seriously?' The girl stared at Eve. 'Oh my word, yes please, I'd love that.'

Eve grinned. 'Consider it done. Just write down your address and I'll get that sorted.'

'How?' the girl asked.

'Because.' Eve reached into her handbag, pulled out her sunglasses and put them on. 'I am Evelyn Lace.'

The girl blinked at her and then checked the photo on the back of the book. 'You are kidding me.'

'Nope. It's true.' Eve took the book from her, turned to the inside cover and signed it 'Best wishes Evelyn Lace'.

Eve sat back, expecting the girl to explode with excitement. But Eve was in for a surprise.

'I do not believe it,' the girl said, with a huff. 'You just sat there and let me take abuse from that awful woman. She called both of us filthy. You didn't stand up for me, or yourself, or your own books. So much for giving other women confidence and empowerment. You're as bad as she is. In fact, no, you're worse. You lied to her.'

'I . . . I didn't think of it like that,' Eve stammered.

'Are you ashamed of what you write?' the girl demanded.

'No, not at all,' Eve protested. 'I just prefer to keep a low profile.'

But Eve was lying, wasn't she? Because she was ashamed, which was why no one, not even her best friend, knew that she was bestselling author Evelyn Lace. If she couldn't stand up and defend her books, why should anyone else? Eve felt herself blush with guilt.

'Whatever.' The girl packed up her things angrily. 'Do you know something? You were such a role model to me until now. I grew up afraid to express myself, afraid to be who I really am. These books gave me the confidence to say what I want. But now I realise you're a fake. You just lost yourself a reader. And you can keep this.' She pushed the signed book back towards Eve, 'I don't want it. Excuse me, I'm moving seats.'

'Where is she going? What have I missed?' asked the old man, returning just in time to see the girl stomp off. But before Eve could come up with a good answer, her publicist Gemma called again.

'There's a major problem with the trains apparently – one of my other authors is also stuck. I doubt you're going to get to the printers on time, so you'll have to abandon the visit. Never mind, let's not lose the opportunity to shout about the new book. Can you do an Instagram story about your disastrous journey and give away a signed copy on your Facebook page instead? Oh no, my other author is trying to get through.'

'Sure, I can do an Instagram story,' Eve said, 'but couldn't you do the giveaway for me—' Eve looked at her phone; the line was dead. Gemma must have picked up her other call. Great, now she had even more work to do. It was times like these when Eve could do with an assistant to help her out.

The train manager came back with further news. 'Attention all passengers. We regret to inform you that this service will terminate here due to a major incident affecting all trains which will take several hours to clear. Please gather up your luggage and leave this service as soon as possible.'

The old man caught her eye. 'Now what are we going to do?'

Eve knew exactly what she wanted to do. After such a terrible journey, what she craved more than anything was a hug and the chance to catch up with one of her favourite people in the whole world: Jo. She didn't care if Jo asked her awkward questions; she'd think of an answer. She simply didn't want to avoid her best friend anymore.

She opened Jo's contact details on her phone. It had taken Eve ages to get Jo's new address out of her when they'd moved two years ago. All she'd wanted to do was send her a house-warming present, but Jo had said there was no need. That was Jo all over: totally selfless. Eve had never missed her more.

'I don't know about you,' said Eve to the old man, opening her Uber account to order a taxi. 'But I haven't seen my best friend in a long time, and I think this is fate's way of telling me that it's time I did.'

Chapter Four

Jo was scrubbing the oven shelves with wire wool when the doorbell rang. It was probably another delivery for Maria's birthday, she thought, pulling the plug out of the sink. Maria was lucky that Jo was still here to take in the parcel. She should have gone home by now, but as she didn't have anything to rush off for, and Maria had asked her to do some extra cleaning, she'd decided to stay.

'Coming!' She pushed her hair off her sweaty forehead with the back of her hand and rushed to answer the door, peeling off her rubber gloves as she went.

'Sorry I was...'

Jo opened the door mid-sentence, and the words died on her lips. For a split-second she thought she was seeing things. She blinked to double check, but no, it was definitely Eve. She was really here, standing on the doorstep. *Maria's* doorstep. Except of course, that Eve thought it was Jo's doorstep.

'Surprise!' Eve flung out her arms.

'You can say that again.' Jo felt dizzy with panic.

'OK. Surprise!' Eve repeated, laughing at her own joke.

'You didn't mention anything about visiting on the phone.' Jo swallowed. What was she going to do? Welcome her in and pretend? Or confess that this wasn't her house immediately, get it over with?

'I didn't know myself then,' Eve beamed. 'It was a surprise to me too.'

'And you had my address with you?' Jo laughed nervously.

'Of course. On my phone, like all my important stuff.'

Jo had tried to avoid giving Eve her address, making up excuses for not needing presents when they moved in, and asking for a cinema voucher which could be emailed for her birthday. She had been worried that Eve might look up their new street online and then ask why the vicar had been allocated such a small house when their previous homes had been large.

But there had been no getting around Faith's birthday. Eve was her godmother and insisted on sending a proper present. In the end, Jo had asked Maria if she could arrange to have Faith's birthday parcels sent to this address to prevent her daughter from spotting them before the big day.

'So how cool is this!' Eve continued, her arms spread wide. 'Are you pleased to see me?'

'Yes,' Jo blurted out firmly. Because it was true. She was pleased, but also scared to death. She didn't have the nerve for this sort of deception. It was one thing lying to her friend on text or in phone calls, but now Eve was here, in person, Jo was going to find it very difficult not to crumble under the pressure of it all and tell her the truth.

'Sure about that?' said Eve.

'Very sure.' Jo felt ashamed of herself for not giving Eve a proper welcome. She hugged her and Eve held her tight. 'It is really lovely to see you.'

Jo needed that hug. She didn't get held much these days. She felt all choked up.

'Same. I've missed you,' Eve mumbled into her shoulder.

'Me too.' Jo sniffed away tears and took a step back to look at Eve. 'So what brings you here so unexpectedly?'

'The train I was on got cancelled and we all had to get off. Imagine my surprise when I realised I was in Boddington.'

'Imagine!' Jo said weakly.

Eve began to tell her about the major train

disruption, but all Jo could focus on was that the lies she had told her best friend were about to get her in the biggest tangle of her life.

'What are the chances that I'd accidentally end up in your neighbourhood?' said Eve. 'It felt as if the universe was bringing us together.'

'It does seem like an impossible coincidence,' said Jo uneasily.

'And I thought, what would I rather do: wait for a replacement bus for hours, or take the opportunity to see my oldest friend?' Eve shrugged happily. 'It was a no-brainer. I was going to phone first, but then I thought it would be fun to turn up unannounced so here I am. Ta-da!'

Fun wasn't quite how Jo would describe it, but Eve was here now, so she was just going to have to manage the situation as best as she could. And it was really good to see her.

'I'm afraid I haven't got a car.' Jo pulled a face. 'So I won't be able to drive you wherever it is you need to go.'

'I wasn't expecting a lift. I can get a taxi. I just thought we could have a catch-up over coffee?' Eve peered over Jo's shoulder, looking down the hall and then back to Jo.

Jo's heart thumped; Eve was expecting to be invited in. But Eve would take one look at Maria's house and the game would be up. There was no way Jo would be able to pass Maria's house off as her own.

'That's a lovely idea, but I was just on my way out.' Jo pulled the door towards her, blocking Eve's view.

'I see.' Eve stared at the rubber gloves in Jo's hand. 'I've obviously called at a bad time, I should leave, let you get on with . . . going out.'

Jo hesitated, feeling like the worst person in the world. That would definitely be the easiest thing. But she couldn't send her oldest friend away just to make things easier for herself. Besides it would be great to have a catch-up. If only she could think of a way to do it without having to confess that this wasn't her house after all.

Jo gave the gloves a wave. 'I've just finished cleaning the oven, that's why I look such a mess.'

Eve giggled. 'I did wonder. You dress so neatly usually. I don't think I've ever seen you so . . . casual.'

Jo glanced down at her cleaning clothes. There were sweat patches under the arms of her T-shirt and her jeans had been splashed with greasy water. Her trainers were worn, but at least they were fairly clean.

'A dress, shoes, earrings, and nail polish to

34

match your outfit,' Eve continued. 'I've always been the scruff in jeans.'

'You were never scruffy, you were always the cool one,' Jo argued, folding her arms to hide the worst of the armpit situation. 'You still are, and you look incredible. Young and trendy. And all in black, that's a new look for you.'

There was something else different about Eve that Jo couldn't quite put a finger on. A new gloss to her demeanour. Her hair was shinier, her teeth were whiter, her leather jacket looked expensive and her handbag... Jo did a double take. 'Nice designer bag!'

'Oh, thanks.' Eve looked down at the floor. 'It's a fake. Bought it from the market. So...?'

'So what?' Jo waited.

'Aren't you going to invite me in?' Eve twinkled her eyes. 'Or are you rushing off right now?'

'I know, let's go out for lunch,' Jo suggested on a whim. 'Unless you don't have time?'

Eve shook her head. 'I'm not in a hurry. My publicist, I mean my er...' She ran a hand through her hair. 'Public transport, um, thingy. Never mind. Basically, I've cancelled my appointment.'

'That's a shame,' said Jo, although she had no idea what Eve was talking about. 'You didn't say where you were heading?'

'I had an appointment with . . .' Eve ran her tongue around her teeth as if her mouth had gone dry. 'Someone. Family in Suffolk.'

Eve seemed more nervous to Jo than usual. Perhaps it was because they hadn't seen each other for so long and Jo hadn't exactly been very welcoming.

'Can I get you—?' Jo stopped. She had been about to offer Eve a glass of water before remembering that that would mean letting her inside Maria's house. 'I never knew you had family in Suffolk. Amazing that we can still find out new information about each other after all these years!'

As soon as Jo had spoken, she realised the irony in her words. There were so many new things which she had been keeping from Eve.

'Really amazing.' Eve's words came out as a croak. A blush spread from her cheeks all the way down her neck. 'Anyway, lunch sounds great. My treat. I'll wait while you go and get changed.'

'Changed? You mean put on different clothes? Right now?' Jo blinked at her. How was she going to produce another outfit while she was at Maria's house without access to her own wardrobe? This was getting more complicated by the second.

'Jo, we're going out for lunch,' Eve giggled.

'I'm going to go wild and order us champagne to celebrate twenty-five years of our friendship. Call me fussy, but you can't go out dressed like a cleaner.'

Jo bristled. 'What's wrong with dressing like a cleaner?'

'Nothing when you're actually cleaning.' Eve gave her a gentle shove into the house. 'Go on, upstairs and I'll go to the loo while I'm waiting.' She bypassed Jo and walked along the hallway where she stopped, open-mouthed and stared. 'Wow.'

'What's the matter?' Jo's skin prickled as Eve turned a full circle, taking in every detail of the hallway which was decorated in Maria's ultra-glamorous style.

Eve said nothing for a long moment, her eyes finally settling on Jo with such an intense look that Jo felt herself grow hot. 'This is... very nice, very different to your old house. Not what I was expecting. Is this the bathroom?' She opened a door and poked her head inside. 'Oh yes, here we are. Go on then, Jo, get changed. I'm starving.'

Eve shut the bathroom door behind her and Jo heard her let out a long breath.

Jo leant her head against the wall for a moment, to gather her thoughts. Not only was Eve now loose in Maria's house, a situation which Jo had been trying her hardest to avoid, but Eve was expecting her to change into fresh clothes. The only clothes here belonged to her boss.

'Why, oh why, does life have to be so complicated?' muttered Jo under her breath.

Chapter Five

As Eve locked the bathroom door, she heard Jo call to her.

'I'll be as quick as I can. Wait for me right here in the hall, OK?'

'Will do,' Eve replied. 'No need to rush.'

Eve was quite glad of a chance to catch her breath. She'd only been here five minutes, and she'd almost let the cat out of the bag several times about her new career. Her *publicist*, for goodness sake, what had she been thinking? Luckily, Jo hadn't commented when she'd quickly changed it to public transport, but she must have wondered what Eve was talking about.

Eve splashed cold water on her face to cool her cheeks down. She and Jo used to be so at ease with each other. Whenever they'd get together, they'd slip straight into the banter which had always been part of their friendship, laughing and teasing each other, having fun in each other's company. Perhaps Jo could tell that Eve was keeping secrets and that was making her edgy too.

In spite of the awkwardness, Eve was glad she had come, even if Jo had taken some persuading to go for lunch. At one point, Eve had thought Jo wasn't going to let her into the house at all.

Maybe Duncan was at home somewhere working, and Jo was concerned about disturbing him. Jo had nothing to worry about there, Eve was only too happy to avoid him. There was something about Jo's husband which gave Eve the shivers. Jo was always on edge when he was around, as if she couldn't relax in her own home. Secretly, Eve thought that Jo would be much better off without him. Not that Eve would ever dream of saying as much. Jo loved him, and that was all that mattered.

Eve snorted with surprise when she noticed the leopard print toilet seat. That wasn't Jo's usual taste. Or leopard print towels. In fact, the whole bathroom felt very unlike Jo: the mirror with lights set around it reminded Eve of being in a theatre dressing room. Then there were the glittery tiles around the basin and the fabric blind at the window with actual leopards printed on it.

Eve went to the loo, washed her hands and emerged into the hall to wait for Jo as instructed. The entrance hall had taken Eve by surprise too;

Jo's interior style had really changed since they'd moved into this house. No wonder Jo had been cleaning when she arrived, she must spend half her life keeping the place spotless. Glossy marble floor, crystal chandelier overhead, the glass table on which sat the flowers Jo had sent a picture of earlier and behind them, a giant mirror. Every surface gleamed. The house felt more like it had been designed by a footballer's wife, not a vicar's wife. If Eve was honest, she preferred Jo's last house, which had been homely and cosy.

It dawned on Eve that Jo had never sent her photos of a whole room since she'd moved in. It was always a close-up of tiny details, so it felt very odd to be finally seeing the real thing for herself.

Three doors led from the hall, one slightly open to the kitchen, the other two closed. Eve was itching to explore. Surely Jo wouldn't mind if she had a look around? She strained to listen for Duncan's voice in case he was on the phone, but she couldn't hear a sound.

Eve checked that Jo wasn't coming down the stairs and gently eased open one of the closed doors so as to not make a noise. As soon as it was open, something furry shot out and brushed against her leg.

'Oh my God!' She leapt back in shock as a

long-haired tabby cat skittered past her and into the kitchen.

'What's the matter, what's happened?' Jo yelled from upstairs.

Eve slammed the door shut guiltily just as Jo came into view at the top of the banister. She appeared to be trapped inside a leopard print satin shirt, her face mostly hidden, her left arm wedged above her head and all her bra showing.

Eve pressed a hand to her mouth and tried not to giggle. 'I was just charged at by a cat.'

'Whoops!' Jo panted. 'I must have shut Fergus into the living room by mistake.'

'You've got a cat?' said Eve; it was hard to keep a straight face watching Jo wriggling inside her shirt. She recalled how Faith had always wanted a pet, but was never allowed one. 'I thought Duncan was allergic to cat fur?'

Jo paused in her struggle to make herself decent and peered down at Eve. 'He is. It aggravates his asthma. That's not my cat.'

There was a squeak followed by a thud from the kitchen.

'Is there a cat flap in the kitchen?' Eve asked.

'Er. Yes.' Using her free hand, Jo managed to tug the top down over her ribs.

'Even though you don't have a cat?'

'It was here when we moved in,' Jo explained.

'That cat is a menace, it's always hanging around here looking for food.'

'Do you want a hand?' Eve offered, taking a step towards the staircase. Poor Jo was looking a bit red faced with the effort.

'No!' Jo yelped. 'Stay down there!'

'All right, keep your hair on.' Eve held her hands up in defence. Jo was acting very weirdly. 'If you're sure.'

'Yep, I've almost done it.' Jo gave the top a sharp tug and the fabric tore as she forced her elbow through the armhole. 'Oh, you are kidding me. Now what am I going to do?'

'Choose another top?' Eve winced. 'Perhaps something a bit looser?'

'That was the only one that fit,' Jo murmured softly.

'What on earth are you talking about? Surely all your clothes fit? OK,' said Eve firmly. 'I'm coming up and you're going to let me help you.'

'Don't do that!' Jo yelled. 'I'll come down.'

Before Eve could take another step, Jo flung herself down the stairs, with one arm still stuck above her head.

'Jo!' Eve gasped. 'Be careful, you'll fall!'

'I'm fine.' Jo stopped in front of Eve and bent down. 'If you pull up from the hem, the whole thing should come off.'

Eve gingerly removed the satin shirt and peeked at the label. Size extra small! No wonder it was a snug fit. Jo had a lovely figure, but she had never been petite.

Jo covered her chest with her arm. 'Sorry about flashing my sexy sports bra. It's the most practical thing for when I'm cleaning.'

'Oh I agree, I've got a Sweaty Betty one I wear when I'm working out with my personal trainer,' said Eve. 'Nothing moves when I'm in that.'

Jo's eyes widened. 'You've got a personal trainer? Isn't that very expensive?'

'It was a special offer at the gym.' Eve delved into her bag on the pretext of checking her phone to hide her blushing face. She didn't mean to mention that she had a personal trainer. 'I'll read my emails while you finish getting changed, if you don't mind.'

'OK. Stay right there, I'll grab something else.'

'Don't worry, I won't disturb Duncan,' said Eve. 'I presume that's why you want me to stay in the hall?'

'Sorry, you must think I'm being very rude,' said Jo, looking guilty. 'But yes, he's in the office, working on his sermon for Sunday.'

'Understood.' Eve was relieved, she didn't want to see him anyway. 'We'll just say goodbye to him before we leave.'

'That might not be such a good idea,' Jo stammered.

Just then Eve's phone beeped with a message from Gemma, and she shielded the screen from Jo. 'If you're sure,' she said distractedly and clicked on the message.

Ring me ASAP! Brilliant press opportunity but we need to act fast! EEEK!

Eve's chest fluttered with excitement. She wondered what it could be. She also wondered how on earth she could phone her publicist without Jo hearing her. She daren't open another door, not after the last time. She'd have to go out into the front garden.

'Jo?' she shouted up the stairs. 'I'll wait on the porch. Just need to make a call.'

'OK,' came the response in a wobbly voice. It almost sounded as if Jo was about to cry, but that couldn't be the case, could it?

Chapter Six

Upstairs in Maria's bedroom, Jo examined the torn seam on Maria's blouse and tried not to panic. What had possessed her to put on something so fitted when Maria was so much slimmer than her? Eve turning up out of the blue had thrown her into a spin and she was behaving completely out of character. Even with her very best attempt at sewing up the seam, it would never be an invisible mend. But there was nothing she could do now, other than simply put it away. She felt awful about it.

Jo flicked through the wardrobe again and settled on a stretchy black jersey dress that she'd never seen Maria wear. It was probably a bit too formal for lunch in a café, but her trainers did a good job of making the outfit more casual.

Jo put it on and covered up her old sports bra. She remembered Eve's comment about Sweaty Betty. That brand was expensive. And having a personal trainer was *really* expensive. Where was Eve's money coming from all of a sudden?

What was she not telling her? Her friend seemed different in lots of little ways; Jo was going to have to do some digging over lunch and find out what was going on in her life.

Jo caught sight of her reflection on the way out of the room and yelped in shock. Her hairline was damp with sweat and without any mascara on, her eyes looked like tiny dots in her flushed face. She quickly ran Maria's hairbrush through her hair, found some mascara in the dressing table and, finally, helped herself to a spritz of perfume.

She didn't look anywhere nearly as smart as Eve, but it would have to do. They needed to leave the house as soon as possible before Eve asked any more questions about Duncan. She closed the bedroom door and headed along the landing. She got halfway down the stairs when her phone rang.

It was her daughter, Faith.

'Hi darling!' said Jo. 'How are—?'

'Mum!' Faith interrupted. 'Thank heavens, I need help. It's an emergency.'

The words every parent dreads. Jo's heart dropped in an instant. 'What's happened?'

'I've got a job interview in an hour's time.'

'You frightened the life out of me!' Jo clutched her chest. 'Congratulations! I thought for a moment—'

'Sorry Mum, I haven't got time to chat.' Faith sounded breathy with panic. 'I'll tell you later. They told me to dress smart and my white shirt has got a stain on it. I've tried everything. You're good at this sort of stuff. Can you help?'

'Not really,' she lowered her voice. 'I'm about to leave Maria's and—'

'That's OK. Brad can probably bring me over. Hold on. Brad, can you give me a lift please?' Jo held the phone away from her ear while Faith yelled to her boyfriend.

Brad's muffled voice shouted back that he could. Of course he would. Brad was a lovely boy; Jo approved.

'You can't come here, Faith.' Jo looked over the staircase to check that Eve hadn't come back inside.

'Why not?'

'Because . . .' Jo faltered, unable to tell her daughter the truth. Because Faith had no idea that her mother had been lying to Eve. Faith did not know that Eve thought this was where they lived. With Duncan. 'Look, can't you wear something else?'

'Like what? I haven't got anything else smart,' Faith replied. 'This will take two minutes, OK, we're on our way. See you in five.'

The line went dead. It would be fine, Jo told

herself. All she had to do was get everyone out of the house as quickly as possible. Oh, and stay calm. *Argghhh!*

As Jo reached the bottom of the stairs, Eve burst through the front door, her eyes dancing with excitement.

'Everything OK?' Jo asked.

'Yes!' said Eve, beaming. 'Everything is great. Brilliant. Really good. You look nice. Do you know what, Jo?' Eve threw her arms around her friend. 'I just want to say that I'm really glad I came. It's so nice to see you.'

Jo swallowed the lump in her throat. If she hadn't pretended to her friend that she was the owner of this house instead of its cleaner, if she had only confessed that Duncan had had an affair, embezzled money from the church and done a midnight flit leaving her to face the consequences, she'd be glad that Eve had come too. But instead she felt as if she was teetering on a knife edge. 'It's really nice to see you,' she confirmed. 'And good news! Faith is on her way over, so you can say hello to her too.'

Eve's smile widened. 'My lovely goddaughter! What a bonus.'

'But it does mean we've got to wait a few minutes for her. She's got a laundry emergency, and apparently I'm the only one who can solve it for her.'

'No problem. Actually.' Eve checked her phone. 'I've got another call to take at one o'clock, so that works out well.'

Jo almost sighed with relief; at least this would keep Eve out of the way while Jo worked on Faith's shirt.

'You are in demand!' she said. 'I'm glad business at the driving school is good for you.'

'Oh yes,' Eve said, with a high-pitched laugh. 'So many people. All wanting to learn to drive.'

Was it Jo's imagination, or was Eve squirming a little?

'Now, I don't want to disturb Duncan,' Eve continued, 'but I do need a strong phone signal for this call. Is there a quiet room I can use? I don't think the front garden is going to work.'

'Absolutely! Of course, you must take the call in the house. Um...' Jo tried to think of a place that was least likely to be full of clues that this was not the home of a vicar and his wife.

The trouble was that the house was a true reflection of Maria's personality: all glitz and glamour. The only room which had escaped the animal print and chandeliers treatment was the office, next to the kitchen. Maria's husband, Nigel, often took video calls in there and insisted that it stayed neutral. It wasn't ideal, but at least they could access it without going through the main living rooms.

'Follow me,' said Jo, charging through the kitchen as quickly as she could.

'The décor in this new house is quite a departure from your old one,' Eve commented, trotting behind her to keep up.

'It was like this when I arrived,' said Jo, not untruthfully. 'We've decided to leave it as it is for now while we get to know it. You'll understand when you move into your new house. Where did you say it was?'

'The Cotswolds.' Eve cleared her throat.

Jo glanced back at her. 'How gorgeous! I can't wait to hear all about it.'

Eve averted her eyes and spotted the posh coffee machine. 'Very fancy. I remember when you only drank instant.'

'I still do,' Jo admitted.

'So . . . ?' Eve pointed at the machine.

'I won it in a competition in a magazine,' Jo said, quickly making up another lie.

'Lucky you.' Eve stopped and looked around. 'Wait. I've just realised what's missing from in here. You always used to have a wooden dresser in the kitchen, with your collection of pottery chickens on the shelves.'

Jo thought of her tiny kitchen in the rented house. There hadn't been room for her lovely old dresser. Getting rid of that had been a difficult decision. She still had the chickens lined up on the window sill.

'I sold that,' she said. 'Time for a change.'

'So I see,' Eve chuckled, peering into the conservatory which was tacked onto the side of the kitchen. 'Is that a disco ball on the ceiling in there? And a cocktail cabinet? Who are you and what have you done with my friend?'

Jo did her best to laugh along with Eve.

'We, er . . .' Jo wracked her brains to come up with an excuse. 'The parish has an under-elevens ballroom dancing club. We let them use that space for their Christmas party. Here's the office.'

That had to be her most ridiculous lie yet, she thought, as she opened the door and gestured for Eve to go in.

'A zebra print rug?' Eve stepped gingerly onto the rug which Jo had always despised. 'Was that here when you arrived too?'

'That was a gift.' Jo felt her face heat up and fiddled with her hair to hide her pink cheeks. 'From a parishioner. Duncan once mentioned in a sermon about loving a visit to the zoo as a child.'

'How kind,' said Eve, with a giggle and pointed to a brass lamp on the desk which was shaped like a tree and had a monkey swinging from it. 'And the lamp?'

'Another gift.' Jo was getting more and more flustered with every lie. 'Some people are very generous.'

'Wait a minute.' Eve frowned. 'Didn't you say that Duncan was working in the office?'

'Um ... I did. But now he's not,' said Jo, feeling a line of sweat appear on her upper lip in her discomfort. 'He must have nipped out for a walk through the back garden. There's a gate at the bottom that leads to a path.'

'Without telling you?' Eve didn't look convinced. 'Isn't that a bit unusual?'

'We're not in each other's pockets,' Jo said, trying not to sound defensive.

'No of course not,' said Eve. 'I'm just disappointed that I'm going to miss him.'

Jo softened. That was kind of Eve to say, especially as Duncan had never really made Eve welcome in their home. She almost squeaked in panic as a framed photo of Maria and Nigel on the office desk caught her eye. Damn. She'd forgotten about that. She pulled open a drawer in the desk and slid the picture in, hoping that Eve didn't notice.

'What was that?' Eve asked.

'Oh, er, nothing,' Jo stammered.

'It's a photo of you, isn't it, let's have a look.' Eve's hand reached for the drawer.

'No, don't!' Jo's words came out louder than she'd meant making Eve jump. 'Sorry, but it's a terrible picture of me. I'd rather you didn't look.'

'But—' Eve persisted.

'Do you need the WiFi code at all?' Jo grabbed the router and turned it around so Eve could read the password.

'Oh, yes please.'

She breathed a sigh of relief while Eve put the correct sequence of numbers and letters into her phone.

'Gosh, look at all these books!' Eve commented, noticing the entire wall taken up by bookshelves behind them.

'Yes, they're both big readers,' said Jo.

Maria was always coming back from the shops with the latest bestsellers. Nigel preferred non-fiction. Jo didn't have the space in her new house for books. She'd had to get rid of most of her books when she moved.

'They?' Eve gave her a quizzical look. 'Duncan and Faith, do you mean? What about you?'

'Yes, and me of course,' said Jo. She could have kicked herself for her mistake. She ran her eye across the shelves. Amongst the fiction, there were countless celebrity biographies, reams of travel books and even some poetry. Nothing that she nor the rest of her family would normally read. 'Faith adores poetry. And most of the novels are mine, of course.'

Eve stopped in her tracks and gasped, pointing at a row of books by Maria's favourite author, Evelyn Lace. Jo had never read any, but Maria raved about them.

'What's the matter?' Jo asked.

'These books.' Eve seemed lost for words for a moment and when she spoke, it almost looked as if she had tears in her eyes. 'I'd never have expected to see these here.'

'Why not?' Jo asked. 'They're a good read.'

'Because I cannot imagine Duncan approving of sexy novels.' Eve looked surprised.

'Oh I see.' Jo felt her face heat up. Maria had never told her what they were about, just that she couldn't put them down. 'Duncan's attitude to a lot of things has changed since I last saw you.'

'Care to expand on that?' Eve asked gently.

Jo shook her head, feeling a pang of sorrow that despite the depth of their friendship, she still didn't feel able to tell her the truth. Maybe one day, but not today when things seemed to be going well for Eve. She didn't want to feel Eve's pity.

Before either of them could speak again, the bell rang.

'That will be Faith,' said Jo, gratefully, turning towards the office door.

'Doesn't she have her own key?' Eve said.

'Um.' Jo thought before answering. 'She does, but she's so scatty. She forgets it more often than remembering it. Come back into the kitchen when you've finished on the phone.'

Eve looked at the time on her phone. 'Sure. But make sure Faith doesn't leave without talking to me. I want to speak to at least one other member of your family.'

'Will do,' said Jo, already leaving the room. 'Good luck with your call.'

Jo pulled the office door closed behind her. There was absolutely no way she could let the two of them meet. She would have to wash Faith's shirt and get her out of the house before Faith had the opportunity to tell Eve the truth about what she was really doing in this house with a cat, leopard print furnishings and a shelf full of naughty novels.

The doorbell rang again.

'Coming darling!' Jo took a fortifying breath; the last time she'd felt this on edge, her husband had announced he was leaving her.

Today couldn't be as bad as that, could it?

Chapter Seven

Eve was in shock. Jo was a fan of the books that she had written! She would never have predicted this in a million years. Eve was so happy that she didn't know what to do with herself. Jo Potter, a reader of racy novels. She shook her head as this new knowledge sank in. Jo always used to read much more highbrow stuff. Eve remembered joking on holiday once about how different the two of them were, despite being best friends.

And even more shocking, Duncan, who was usually such a spoilsport, hadn't forbidden her from reading them! It seemed out of character for both of them. Eve ran her finger along the spines of her own books. She had been nervous of admitting to writing these books in case her friends had reacted negatively.

And while Eve had been hiding her identity as an author, her best friend had been reading them. This changed everything. If Eve had been looking for a sign that it was time she confessed to having a secret identity then this had to be it.

Maybe, when this radio interview was done, she would reveal the truth. In fact, she even knew how she should do it. She could sign all these books! This was going to be such fun! She could already imagine the look of surprise on Jo's face. She took one of her books from the shelf, sat down at the desk and took a pen out of her handbag. Turning to the inside front cover, Eve's pen hovered over the page. She'd write a personal dedication to her best friend.

There was a soft knock at the door. Eve quickly stuffed the book under her bag.

'Come in!'

'Aunty Eve!' Her goddaughter flung herself at Eve.

'Look at you, all grown up!' Eve exclaimed, getting up to give her a big hug.

'I am.' Faith's eyes shone. 'With a job interview any second. You look amazing, by the way. Very foxy. Have you had work done?'

'Faith!' Jo gasped, hurtling into the office after her daughter. 'Sorry, Eve.'

'It's fine.' Eve felt herself go red. 'I'll be honest, I have had a bit of Botox, just to smooth out some of the wrinkles. But really, I've started taking more care with my appearance.'

'Something you ought to try, young lady,' Jo

said. 'Talking of which, we should sort that shirt out.'

'Ugh,' Faith pouted. 'Can't you do it while I chat to Eve?'

'No,' said Jo briskly.

Eve's phone started to ring. 'I'd better get this.'

'Come on Faith.' Jo ushered her daughter out of the room.

Eve answered her phone. It was Gemma on the line.

'OK. Here's the thing.' There was a nervous laugh in Gemma's voice. 'Your interview is going to be on today's *Book Lovers Show* on Radio Britain.'

Eve let out a squeal. 'Today? Live?'

'Yes!' gushed Gemma.

'Oh my goodness.' Eve's chest rose with pride. She listened to this programme every week; it was a dream come true to be interviewed on it. 'Thank you.'

'You're welcome, this is one of the best pieces of PR I've ever done in my life,' Gemma continued, 'I'm so excited. No swearing and try to avoid saying "um" and "er".'

'I think I can manage that,' said Eve, although she felt a flicker of nerves at the thought of it. 'It's time to show the book world that spicy fiction shouldn't be a dirty secret. It's a way for women to express themselves, take control, have confidence.'

'Good for you! But don't read any juicy bits out on air. Children might be listening. And my mum.' Gemma giggled. 'I've already told her that one of my authors is going on the radio.'

'Understood. I won't let you down, Gemma,' said Eve, wishing her own mum was still alive. She'd have listened in too, and been proud of her daughter. But at least now that Eve knew Jo was a fan, she was sure that Jo would be proud, too. What a fool she had been, to think that Jo wouldn't support her. Eve should have been brave enough to trust her. Just because that woman on the train had been horrible, it didn't mean that others would feel the same way. No, Jo would always be her biggest cheerleader. The thought perked her up.

Gemma told her that the show was running a minute or so behind schedule, but the producer would be in touch very soon and Eve was to be ready for the call.

Eve promised she would. She turned up the volume on her phone so that she wouldn't miss it when it rang and opened the office door into the kitchen.

Jo was at the far end of the room running water into the sink. Faith was singing along to the radio and doing a dance with Fergus the cat who had clearly found his way back inside.

Eve was about to join them when Jo spoke.

'Have you read anything by Evelyn Lace, darling?'

'No,' said Faith, putting the cat down on the floor. 'But loads of my friends have. I'm completely addicted to thrillers, that's why I've got so many of them. Why?'

Not poetry, then, as Jo had said.

'Do you know if they're . . .' Jo lowered her voice. 'Rude?'

Eve frowned. How bizarre. Jo was asking her daughter about the books as if she'd never read them. Something about this conversation felt odd. Eve stepped backwards into the office and peered around the door. She wanted to listen without them knowing she was there.

Faith shrugged. 'If you consider sex between consenting adults rude, then I guess so. I don't. People are weird: read a book about mass murderers and no one bats an eyelid; read a book about something completely normal like sex and people freak out.'

Eve bit back a smile; *yes, Faith, good answer*.

'Oh gosh,' said Jo. 'I had no idea they had sex in them.'

'Mum,' Faith giggled. 'You are so sweet, of

course you wouldn't know. Dad wouldn't allow them into the house?'

OK, now Eve was really confused. If Duncan would forbid them, why were there a collection of them right under his nose in his office? Why had Jo said she'd read them when she clearly hadn't? And if some of the books on the shelves belonged to Faith, where were her thrillers?

'Darling, even if I do get this mark out of your shirt, I doubt it'll dry in time,' Jo said with a sigh.

'It's fine. I'll use my hair straighteners on it to dry it fast,' Faith replied, opening up kitchen cupboards. 'Where does she keep the stain remover?'

'Next to the detergent. She uses that expensive stuff in the pink tub.'

She? Who were they referring to? This was getting stranger and stranger. Surely Faith would know where to find the laundry products in her own home. Lots of things didn't add up. There was the whole issue of the style of the house. Then there was Faith apparently not having a key to the front door. Plus, Eve had felt an odd vibe from Jo ever since she'd set foot in the house, as if she was nervous about Eve being here. She was going to do some detective work while Faith and Jo were occupied. She had to know what was going on.

Eve tiptoed to the desk and opened the drawer where Jo had shoved that picture frame that had been on display when they'd first walked in. It was a terrible picture of her, according to Jo. Eve pulled it out to look at it and gasped.

A glamorous couple with dazzling white teeth, deep suntans and each holding cocktails grinned out at her. The man was a handsome silver fox, his shirt open to reveal a chunky gold chain. Unless Duncan had had a hair transplant and a facelift, it wasn't him. The woman was all pointy chin and cheekbones, wore a figure-hugging leopard print dress and earrings shaped like disco balls. It definitely wasn't Jo.

For some reason, Jo and Duncan had a photograph of another couple in pride of place on their desk. Why would that be?

Eve's brain raced. She felt as if she was in the middle of that TV show where you had to guess the celebrity house you were in. The footballer's wife interior décor, the cat, the books nobody had read and, she realised suddenly, absolutely nothing to do with Duncan's job in the church – no bibles, no bags of jumble in the hall, no crucifixes on the walls and, crucially, absolutely no evidence of Duncan.

Eve sank down onto the chair. There was only one possible explanation for it all. This house did not belong to Jo and Duncan.

Eve's phone rang at full volume, startling her, and she lunged at it. 'Hello?'

'Evelyn Lace?' said a woman. 'I'm Angela, producer of the *Book Lovers Show*. Are you ready to go live on air?'

'Yes!' Eve squeaked, her mouth suddenly dry with nerves.

'Now just to check,' said Angela. 'There isn't a radio on nearby is there? We have to avoid feedback.'

Eve could hear the radio clearly in the kitchen. Her heart sank. 'I think there might be, yes.'

'Nip and turn it off, and we'll come straight to you in two minutes after the news bulletin.'

Eve let out a sigh. How was she going to persuade Jo to turn off the radio without looking rude?

Chapter Eight

Jo was scrubbing away at the stain on Faith's shirt so hard that she was beginning to sweat. The stain remover wasn't having any effect.

'What am I going to do?' Faith wailed, peering over her shoulder. 'I haven't got time to hang around. Brad's waiting outside and he's having to turn down delivery jobs for this.'

Brad was a student and had several jobs to help fund his studies, one of which was as a fast-food delivery driver.

'I'm doing my best. If all else fails, you'll have to borrow something from upstairs.' Jo flicked a glance over Faith. She would be able to fit into one of Maria's shirts. There must be a plain white one amongst all the animal print. It wasn't the ideal solution. Jo had already torn one of her boss's tops, and Faith was famous for spilling stuff down her own clothes.

Faith groaned. 'I suppose I could, but won't she mind?'

'She?' said Eve appearing suddenly from the office. 'Don't you mean you?'

Faith shook her head. 'No, I mean—'

'What is this, red wine?' Jo raised her voice to drown out Faith before she blurted out Maria's name.

'It's from a leaky pen,' Faith replied.

'Put hairspray on it,' said Eve. 'Usually works for me, I'm forever getting red ink on the cuffs of my shirts.'

'Are you?' Jo gave Eve a curious look. That seemed a very unusual thing to be *forever* happening.

'Well.' Eve rubbed the back of her neck awkwardly. 'Now and then.'

'Thanks Aunty Eve. I've got some with me,' Faith pulled a slim can out of her bag and handed it to her mum.

'Here goes,' said Jo, trying to hide her doubts as she doused the shirt in hairspray.

'Um, I'm really sorry to be rude,' Eve said with an embarrassed laugh. 'But can you turn the radio off, it's disturbing my call.'

'Whoops, sorry.' Jo reached for the radio and turned the volume down. 'There, we'll be as quiet as mice.'

The cat started to miaow and weave in and out of Faith's legs.

'Shush, Fergus,' said Faith, 'you need to be as quiet as a mouse too. Are you hungry?'

Eve winced. 'I mean properly off. It's something to do with feedback. I don't understand it but...'

Jo's heart sank as Faith took a handful of cat biscuits from the tub on the counter and put them in Fergus's bowl.

'That happened to Duncan once when he was interviewed on the radio,' said Jo, wafting Faith's shirt in the air elaborately to distract Eve from watching the cat. 'I didn't realise it was the same for phone calls.'

'Don't ask me. Apologies for being a pain.' Eve turned the radio off herself. 'Jo, that cat bowl says Fergus on it. But you said he isn't your cat.'

'I know, it's so cute, isn't it?' Faith bent down to rub the cat's head. 'He's such a lovely boy. Mum, we should get a kitten.'

Eve was looking at Jo with her eyes narrowed, waiting for an answer.

'Maybe one day,' Jo laughed manically, wishing a hole would appear in the ground and make this nightmare end. 'This hairspray is actually working.'

'Wow!' Faith exclaimed, taking a look herself as Jo ran the tap over the stain to remove the excess hairspray. 'Thanks Aunty Eve, you're a lifesaver. Mum wanted me to borrow something of Maria's.'

Eve fixed Jo with an intense look. 'Maria's?'

Jo swallowed. 'Um. Maria is, Maria is—'

'Mum's boss, duh!' said Faith.

'Right.' Eve nodded slowly. 'And does Maria have a fondness for leopard print by any chance?'

'You noticed?' Faith gave a snort of laughter. 'The woman is obsessed. I mean, can you imagine me turning up to an interview wearing her clothes?'

'Almost as funny as your mum wearing her clothes to go out for lunch.' Eve was still staring at Jo.

'Oh yeah!' Faith looked at Maria's black dress which had had begun to make Jo feel very clammy. 'Why are you wearing that?'

'Because.' Jo's mouth had gone dry. All of her excuses and lies and ridiculous reasons for living here in leopard print luxury instead of a vicarage with clutter and chaos and an awful lot of second-hand furniture escaped her. She tried again. 'Because—'

'And I take it Maria is not only a fan of cats, but of Evelyn Lace books too?' Eve continued.

'Huge fan,' Jo muttered.

'So what if she is?' Faith said defiantly.

Jo ignored her daughter and met Eve's eye. 'I had no idea they were saucy.'

'I'm not interested in that,' said Eve throwing her hands in the air. 'I'm only interested in why you pretended they were yours. Although I was surprised that Duncan had nothing to say about them.'

'As if Mum cares what Dad thinks,' Faith muttered darkly.

'Of course she does.' Eve smiled sadly at her goddaughter. 'Your mum totally stopped wearing short skirts after your dad told her off for revealing too much leg. It's such a shame because she has lovely legs.'

Jo could feel a pulse throbbing in the side of her neck. Everything was slipping out of her control. 'That was a long time ago.'

'Hmm.' Eve chewed the inside of her cheek. 'I'm going to say something here. I might be completely wrong but...'

Jo felt as if she had a stone in the pit of her stomach. 'Please don't say it.'

'This isn't your house, is it?' said Eve.

'Of course not,' Faith sniggered. 'You could fit our entire house into this kitchen.'

'Could you?' Eve pressed a hand to her forehead. 'I don't understand.'

'I'm so sorry,' Jo whispered. Her friend looked so confused. Jo felt awful.

'What's going on here?' Eve asked.

Jo wanted to curl up into a ball and hide. Maybe if she sprayed a cloud of hairspray over herself, she would disappear too like Faith's ink stain. 'It's a long story.'

Faith looked from one of them to the other and frowned. 'Yeah, what is going on? You're both being weird.'

Jo felt as if her entire body was cringing; her face must have been absolutely scarlet. At that moment, Faith's phone rang; she snatched it up and ran out into the garden, talking animatedly. Jo was grateful. The less Faith heard of this conversation the better.

'OK.' Eve folded her arms. 'From the second I arrived something has felt off. I thought you'd be pleased to see me, but instead, it's been as if you're desperate for me to leave. You haven't so much as offered me a glass of water.'

'Do you want a glass of water?' Jo asked.

'No!' Eve shot back. 'What I want is to know what has happened to my friend. You aren't being yourself. And apparently, the address you gave me isn't even for your own house?'

But before anyone had a chance to say anything else, Faith slipped back into the kitchen and a brisk voice spoke from the mobile phone in Eve's hand.

'Thank you, Felicity, for that news update, and coming up next on the *Book Lovers Show*, this afternoon's guest is . . .'

'Shit,' Eve muttered.

'Aunty Eve!' Faith pretended to look shocked. 'No swearing!'

'Keep the radio off,' Eve said flapping her hand at the radio as she strode back towards the office. 'Please. I'd better go and, er, take this call.'

'Yes, of course, we can catch up afterwards.' Jo waited until Eve had closed the door and blew out a shaky breath. So the secret was out – or at least half of it. She had the length of that telephone call to work out what she was going to say to her best friend. The question was, after realising how many lies Jo had told her, would Eve still want to be a friend at all, let alone her best one?

Chapter Nine

Eve stood in the office that she'd been told was Duncan and Jo's, but was in fact Maria's. She was baffled. Why would her best friend withhold the truth? And if this wasn't her house, where did Jo live? Eve didn't know whether to be hurt about the lies or worried. Either way, something very serious must have happened in Jo's life and for whatever reason, she had chosen to not to tell Eve about it. Eve had to find out what was going on.

She didn't really want to do this radio interview now, she wanted to stay focused on Jo. She looked at the phone in her hand. Could she simply hang up and walk away? Too late. A loud voice started up in her ear and the moment was gone.

'Hello and welcome to the *Book Lovers Show*, where we shine a light on what's good and, perhaps more interestingly in today's show, what's bad about the books we read.'

Eve's ears pricked up. *What's bad?* She thought

this radio programme was about celebrating writers. An uncomfortable feeling lodged in her stomach.

'I'm Suzy Whitehouse,' the presenter continued. 'Author of *The Shimmer of Light on the Lake*, a novel written from the point of view of a fallen log at the edge of a lake told over one whole decade. I'll be sitting in for your usual host. This is my first time presenting a radio programme, so go easy on me!'

The *usual* host was a lovely lady called Fiona who Eve knew loved romance novels. She had never heard of Suzy Whitehouse, or her book, which didn't sound like much fun. Never mind, being invited onto the show was a huge honour. All she had to do was remember what her own book was about, answer the questions intelligently and hope that Suzy would talk about the good stuff and not the bad.

'But enough about me,' said Suzy. 'Today, we are joined by a writer whose books tackle a very different genre from mine. Most social media passes me by, but those of you familiar with TikTok may have seen a post today which has gone viral. And the subject of that post is here with us now. Welcome to the show, Evelyn Lace.'

A viral post? Gemma had mentioned nothing about this. What sort of post? TikTok could send an author's sales stratospheric. But it could also do the exact opposite. Which was it? What was going on?

Eve looked at her phone, wondering if she could swipe through to TikTok and look for herself while she was on the call. But she didn't trust herself not to hang up by mistake.

'Evelyn?' Suzy said sharply. 'Are you there?'

'Yes, hello, thank you.' Eve was suddenly nervous, and her tongue felt too large for her mouth. If only she'd accepted a glass of water instead of questioning Jo about her house – or rather *Maria's* house. She gave herself a shake; she needed to stop thinking about Jo and concentrate. Her words came out all thin and weedy. 'It's an absolute pleasure to be here.'

'Readers of your sort of fiction are filthy,' Suzy stated. 'Not my words, of course, but rather the TikTok that's doing the rounds. What do you have to say to that?'

Fear gripped Eve. What could she say? Other than *help*?

Chapter Ten

Faith had plugged in her hair straighteners and was spreading out her shirt on a kitchen towel. 'As if Aunty Eve thinks this is our house,' she giggled.

'I know,' said Jo, weakly. 'I'm not sure how she could have got so confused, but then we haven't seen each other for ages.'

Faith looked up from her task. 'But she must know that since Dad left, we haven't got any money.'

'Hmm,' Jo fiddled with the neck of Maria's dress, avoiding her daughter's gaze.

'And why was she pretending to be on a phone call when she's obviously talking on the radio?'

'Is she?' Jo was taken aback.

Faith sniggered. 'Mum, sometimes, for an intelligent woman, you're incredibly unobservant. The woman was literally introducing Eve as a guest on the *Book Lovers Show*.'

Jo had been so focused on the conversation about Maria that she hadn't really been paying attention. 'I did hear a voice saying something about a news bulletin, but I thought whoever was on the line had the radio on in the background.'

'I didn't even know Aunty Eve was big into books,' said Faith.

'She didn't used to be.' Jo frowned. 'I remember going on holiday with her once. I lay on the beach reading all day while she would listen to music and sing. Badly.'

Just then Faith's phone buzzed again. She picked it up and gave a grunt of annoyance as she read a message on her screen. She began tapping in a reply, leaving Jo to wonder why a driving instructor like Eve would be a guest on a radio show about books. She had to find out, but she didn't want to cause any problems for Eve with feedback. Would it be all right to listen to the radio further away, she wondered?

Jo decided to risk it. She took the radio outside and went to the top of the garden where it couldn't interfere with whatever Eve was doing. She sat down on a garden bench and tried to work out how to retune it to the *Book Lovers Show*. She had just found it when Faith stomped outside, one hand on her hip and her phone in the other hand.

'I don't believe it! I'm so annoyed,' Faith fumed. 'The restaurant has cancelled my interview.

Apparently there's no longer a vacancy. After all that effort!'

'Oh darling, poor you.' Any other time, Jo would have given her daughter her full attention, but she had just heard something on the radio which had blown her mind.

'And now Brad has driven off in a strop because he's had to turn down loads of delivery jobs while he's been sitting outside waiting for me.'

'That's a shame,' said Jo vaguely.

'Mum!' Faith said with a huff. 'Are you listening?'

'Not really, sorry. I'm concentrating on the radio. Listen, is this who I think it is?'

'Aunty Eve?' said Faith.

Jo shook her head in disbelief. 'It does sound like Eve, but apparently it's Evelyn Lace.'

Chapter Eleven

Eve tried to remember what she'd been told about being interviewed on the radio: stand up tall, smile, because people can hear it in your voice when you smile, and speak as if you were talking to a friend. She was already standing, although there was a tremble in her thighs, and when she smiled, her lips kept sticking to her teeth. She could try to speak to Suzy as if they were mates, but she had a feeling that Suzy was less friend than foe.

'We'll come back to that TikTok story in a moment,' said Suzy, after Eve had failed to reply. 'Firstly, congratulations. Your books have been a massive success, selling more than *one million copies* worldwide. Considerably more than *The Shimmer of Light on the Lake.*'

Eve couldn't be sure, but it sounded as if Suzy was amazed that books by Evelyn Lace were so popular. Nonetheless, she plastered on a smile before replying.

'Thank you, I'm very fortunate to have found

a large number of loyal readers.' Eve turned to view the row of her own books on the bookshelf. They were organised from oldest to newest. Maria really was a dedicated fan.

'Indeed!' Suzy said haughtily. 'And yet people have criticised the writing. What do you say to the haters?'

Eve flinched, but laughed politely. 'Haters? That is a bit strong.'

'Well, we writers have to have a thick skin, don't we?' Suzy said, gloomily. 'Book reviewers can be brutal sometimes.'

It sounded as if Suzy had been on the receiving end of some negative reviews herself, thought Eve with a pang of sympathy. Poor thing. It wasn't a nice feeling.

'We can't please everyone with every book. It's important to remember that,' Eve replied kindly.

'Does it bother you that some readers say that your novels are predictable?' Suzy continued, ignoring Eve's gentle advice.

'There is a predictability about most genres,' Eve responded mildly. 'Romcoms have happy endings, the detective always finds the thief in crime books. My erotic romance is no different. I don't think there's anything wrong with delivering what readers want.'

'Oh, absolutely!' Suzy laughed. 'Although you're unlikely to find an Evelyn Lace novel shortlisted for any awards.'

'Not true, actually,' Eve contested. '*Midnight Secret Date* won the Romance Readers Hot Heroes award this year.'

There was a noise from the studio that sounded like a snort of derision. Eve felt her pulse race; she wasn't sure how to handle criticism and still manage to sound positive and cheerful.

'Bravo! I was referring to literary awards, but that is still quite the achievement,' Suzy laughed. 'Now, Evelyn Lace is your pen name, I understand. Why did you decide not to put your own name on the front of your books?'

'I kept my first name but changed my surname. There's another author who writes as my real full name and I didn't want us to get mistaken for one another.' Finally, a question Eve could answer with confidence.

'And I guess hiding behind a fake name also means your friends won't find out what sort of stories are going on in your head,' Suzy pointed out.

'I wouldn't call it hiding,' Eve protested. 'But I prefer to keep my private and professional lives separate. Having a different name helps me to do that.'

'I understand,' said Suzy. 'I've told everyone I know that I've written a book. I'm just so proud of it. Did I mention the title? It's called *The Shimmer of Light on the Lake*. I imagine it would be easier to tell people what you've written if the content wasn't quite so saucy?'

Suzy's words were like a sucker punch to her stomach. Eve could hardly argue, because Suzy was right. Eve had been scared of the reaction of others. It was why she wore sunglasses and bright red lipstick in all her author photos, so that no one would recognise her as Eve Langton.

But it wasn't just about the type of books she wrote, she realised. It was about something else, something much more personal. Because despite her achievements, and the popularity of her books, she still didn't think that she deserved her success. She was waiting for the moment when someone told her that it was all a hoax, and she wasn't a successful author at all. And now, live on air, her worst fears were coming true.

'To tell you the truth, Suzy, when I wrote my first book, I was too nervous to tell anyone because I didn't have confidence in myself. How could I, Eve Lang...' Eve caught herself just in time, before revealing her real name. *Phew, that was close*, she thought. 'How could the girl who didn't do well at school be clever enough to write books?' She hesitated, swallowing the lump in her throat. 'I still feel like that.'

Chapter Twelve

'Oh my god. Evelyn Lace, Eve Langton...' Faith gasped. 'It's Aunty Eve. No wonder she wanted the radio to be switched off.'

'Eve, a famous author.' Jo was numb with shock. 'And she's in Maria's office right now being interviewed live on the radio.' It was so exciting; she'd never known an author before, and this one was her best friend. But Eve had kept it a secret from her. Jo felt a lump in her throat; why would she do that?

Faith whistled. 'Those books are super spicy. I can't wait to tell the group chat that my god-mother is Evelyn Lace, they are going to go wild.' Her eyes sparkled. 'I've just had a thought; that's everyone's birthday presents sorted forever – a signed copy of Aunty Eve's latest book. I've got to go and tell my friends.'

Jo shushed her daughter. 'I can't hear.'

Faith headed back inside with her phone and Jo turned up the volume to listen.

'Imposter syndrome,' said the presenter. 'Very

common amongst people who sell well regardless of literary merit. It is quite frustrating to have studied hard, crafted an intellectual, elegant novel and to only sell a few hundred copies. It's very tough when other writers seem to be able to churn out books every couple of months and hit the bestseller list.'

Jo bristled on Eve's behalf. Suzy Whitehouse was being very mean to her guest. Jo had borrowed Suzy's book from the library a few months ago and enjoyed it. She had even left a glowing review on Amazon. But Suzy didn't sound like a very nice person. She had a good mind to delete it now.

'I believe that comparison is the thief of joy, so—' Eve replied.

'Always easier to live by that motto when you're doing well,' Suzy said abruptly.

Jo tutted at the radio. Suzy wouldn't even let Eve finish her sentence; she was behaving as if she was jealous of Eve's success.

'Now,' Suzy went on, 'what the listeners want to know is how much of your own – how shall I put it – romantic liaisons have you drawn upon? I mean you must have done your research somewhere. Will your partners recognise themselves on the pages of an Evelyn Lace book?'

Jo's jaw dropped. The presenter had gone too far this time. Surely, she couldn't get away with asking those sorts of questions? Jo felt like storming into the office and stopping the interview to protect her friend.

'Part of the skill of being a fiction author is to make the story feel real. Would you ask a crime writer the same question?' Jo clapped as Eve responded to Suzy brilliantly. 'Does someone have to be a killer to write a murder scene? I hope not. I'm flattered that you think that the sex scenes are well researched, I take it as a compliment.'

Jo's heart swelled with pride. You go, girl, she thought.

'But is it really necessary,' Suzy sounded bemused, 'to have so much of the action taking place in the bedroom? Wouldn't it be more intriguing to leave out the more saucy details and let the reader's imagination fill in the gaps?'

'Oh for . . .' Eve began. To Jo's ears it sounded as if Eve had just stopped herself from replying rudely, but she could tell that Suzy was testing her patience. 'The pre-orders for my next book are higher than ever, which tells me that I'm getting the balance right. My goddaughter made a good point today: she said if you read a book about mass murderers no one bats an eyelid, but read a book about something completely normal like sex and people go all weird about it. Feedback like that gives me an enormous sense of pride and it has been one of the best and one of the most unexpected parts of being a published author.'

Jo nodded. There was absolutely no doubt now that Eve was Evelyn Lace. She must have heard her talking to Faith in the kitchen.

'But it isn't just about the story,' Eve went on. 'In fact only today, one of my readers said that my books had given her the courage to express herself and be herself. And—'

'Let's get back to people calling you perverted, and your books pure filth,' Suzy interrupted. 'There's a video going viral of someone doing just that. What do you think of it?'

'I haven't seen it,' Eve admitted.

'But you were there, weren't you, on the train today?'

'I, I, I . . .' Eve stuttered.

'Oh dear, our guest author seems to be stuck for words,' said Suzy cattily. 'Now, stay there, Evelyn, because we're going to break for an urgent travel update . . .'

Jo jumped to her feet, picked up the radio and stormed back into the house. No one belittled a friend of hers like that. Jo had been on the receiving end of poor treatment herself and was not about to stand by and watch it happen to someone she loved.

Chapter Thirteen

Eve gritted her teeth. She *was* stuck for words, but only because this interview was so unpleasant. She had expected a lovely gentle conversation about her books and how wonderful her readers were. And instead, she was being pulled apart by another author! And as for a TikTok video, she needed to see what that was all about as soon as possible.

'Thanks, Suzy,' said a male presenter. 'There is widespread chaos on the trains, following a major incident...'

The sound in her ear changed and the producer was back. 'Sorry about this, Evelyn. Some national transport issue we needed to report on. Won't be long.'

'OK,' Eve replied. The line went quiet, and she murmured under her breath, 'Although quite frankly, I've had quite enough of being roasted by Suzy Whitehouse.'

She slumped into the chair behind the desk. The office door slowly opened, and Jo's head appeared through the gap. She was wide-eyed and looked nervous.

'Hello,' Eve whispered.

'You're Evelyn Lace.' Jo crept slowly into the room.

Eve's heart pounded against her ribs. 'Oh god. I... I... am. I know I should have told you, but...' For the second time in as many minutes, Eve couldn't find the right words.

She was terrified that Jo would react as Suzy had implied her friends would: with disapproval. Seeing her again today had made her realise how much she cherished their friendship; she couldn't bear to lose it.

'So according to Google, my best friend is Evelyn Lace, the million-copy-selling author of spicy romance,' Jo read from her phone. 'Translated into fifteen languages and with TV rights to the *Secret Date* series already in production with Netflix. Is that true?'

Eve managed to nod. 'All true.'

'And I knew nothing about it,' Jo said softly.

Eve felt like the worst person on the planet. Although the two of them spoke and messaged each other all the time, she had kept this enormous thing completely hidden: her new career, her alter ego, even the extra money she was now earning.

'This is insane!' Faith yelled, barrelling into the room and almost knocking Eve over with the force of her hug. 'My godmother is famous!'

'Not really,' Eve replied, returning the young woman's hug.

'You are. Haven't you seen the TikTok about Team Smut?' Faith shoved her phone under Eve's nose.

Eve stared at the screen while Faith played the TikTok. The video showed the woman on the train attacking Eve's books, calling them smutty, and telling the girl that she was disgusting. The caption read: So apparently I'm filthy, because I love Evelyn Lace. Hit 'like' if you're with me #TeamSmut.

'Oh my word!' Eve gasped. 'I saw someone with their phone out, I thought they were taking a selfie, but they were obviously filming us.'

'This has been reposted thousands of times, Aunty Eve.' Faith danced on the spot. 'It's got a quarter of a million likes already. So yeah, I'd say that makes you quite famous.'

That explained why the *Book Lovers Show* decided to interview her at short notice, thought Eve.

'What's really important is what your mum thinks of me.' Eve met Jo's gaze timidly. 'Are you very disappointed about my new career?'

Jo's eyes welled with tears. 'Not at all. It's a huge surprise, but I'm very proud. Why would I be disappointed?'

Eve's own eyes felt hot with the effort of not crying. 'Because of your position in the community. What would Duncan's parishioners say if they knew your best friend writes erotic fiction? And what will Duncan say? He might say we're not allowed to be friends anymore, and I couldn't stand that.'

'This again?' Faith rolled her eyes. 'Aunty Eve, Dad has no control over Mum.'

'Really?' Eve was confused. This was the second time Faith had said something like that, but it seemed very unlikely.

'Faith, please,' Jo interrupted, 'wait a second.'

'*Really*,' Faith continued, ignoring her mum. 'We haven't even seen him since—'

'Faith, stop!' yelled Jo. 'Can I speak to Eve in private please.'

'Fine.' Faith held her hands up in surrender. 'I'm going, but I have to say, for women who claim to be best friends, there seems to be a hell of a lot that you haven't told each other.'

Faith started tapping out a message into her phone before she'd even left the office, leaving Eve and Jo facing each other.

'I'm sorry that I kept secrets from you—' said the two women at the same time.

'Me too,' they both said again.

'You go first,' said Eve quickly.

Jo nodded. 'If I must.'

They both jumped as a voice piped up from Eve's phone. 'Putting you back to the studio.'

Eve pulled a face. 'Sorry.'

'I'm Suzy Whitehouse, author of *The Shimmer of Light on the Lake*, and joining me on today's programme is sex sensation, Evelyn Lace.'

'Don't stand for that,' Jo whispered. 'That's not an acceptable way to introduce you.'

Eve looked at Jo nervously. 'Shall I say something?'

Jo nodded.

Adrenaline surged through Eve; Gemma was going to kill her for what she was about to do.

'You flatter me,' said Eve brightly. 'But I'm just an ordinary woman, writing popular books to please thousands of people, and I'd appreciate it if you dialled down some of the sexual references.'

Jo stuck up both thumbs in approval.

'Whoops, bit of a touchy subject there,' Suzy tittered. 'Now, Eve, what do you say to the people who describe your books as "pure filth"?'

'I've never met anyone who's called them that after reading them. However, there seems to be lots of people happy sharing their opinion *before* reading them.'

'You can't blame them,' Suzy scoffed. 'You're never likely to see your books being studied by English students, are you? The lady on the TikTok called them trash.'

Before Eve could respond, Jo grabbed the phone off her. 'Hello, Suzy, this is Evelyn's best friend, Jo.'

'Um, hello.' Suzy gave a wary laugh. 'This is most unusual.'

'Criticising other people's books is not a nice way to behave,' said Jo sternly. 'There is a reader for every book, and a book for every reader. It would be a very boring world if we all liked the same thing, wouldn't it?'

'Yes,' Suzy admitted. 'I suppose it would.'

'For example,' said Jo, 'I've read your book *The Shimmer of Light on the Lake*.'

There was a pause down the line and Eve thought she heard Suzy gulp in panic.

'I thought it was marvellous,' Jo said briskly.

Eve raised her eyebrows. 'Really?'

Jo nodded at her. 'Beautifully written.'

'Well, er, thank you,' Suzy sounded relieved.

'Now, let's have Evelyn back on the line, shall we?'

'Evelyn's books give a lot of pleasure to a lot of people.' Jo ignored Suzy's instruction. 'And I think she should be every bit as proud of writing them as you are of your *one* book.'

'I am writing a second book,' Suzy mumbled. 'But it's proving a little tricky.'

'Do you agree,' Jo asked Suzy, 'that Evelyn should be proud of her achievements?'

'Yes,' said Suzy after a long hesitation. 'She should.'

'Good,' said Jo triumphantly. 'And so am I. That concludes our interview, goodbye.'

Jo ended the call with a stab of her finger and dropped the phone on the desk as if it was burning her. 'Boom.'

'Jo!' said Eve. 'I can't believe you just did that.'

'Me neither.' Jo pressed her hands to her face. 'I don't know what came over me.'

The women looked at each other and laughed and laughed until tears streamed down their faces.

'So Maria is your boss?' Eve said once she'd caught her breath. She cast her mind back to when she'd arrived, and Jo had said she was cleaning the oven.

Jo nodded. 'I'm her cleaner.'

Eve's phone buzzed; the radio station was ringing her back. Eve sent the call to voicemail. This conversation with Jo was far more important. 'Goodness knows what my publicist is going to say about this,' she said, chewing her lip.

'Publicist or public transport?' said Jo slyly.

'You heard that slip of the tongue, then?' Eve asked.

Jo grinned. 'But I was so scared about making mistakes of my own about this house and...' she hesitated, '...about Duncan, that I didn't say anything.'

Eve took Jo's hands, and they smiled at each other, tears of laughter still glinting in their eyes. 'I'm still not sure what's going here, but I think it's time we had a proper chat, don't you?'

Jo heaved a sigh of relief. 'With pleasure. Do you still fancy going out for lunch?'

Eve wrinkled her nose. 'Actually, what I really want to do, is sit down where no one else can hear us and find out what has been going in your life since the last time I saw you.'

'And I want to find out how little Eve Langton, who I can't ever remember reading a single book, became a bestselling novelist,' said Jo.

'Deal,' said Eve. 'Now get the kettle on and I'll tell all.'

'Even the rude bits?'

Eve nudged Jo towards the door. 'Especially the rude bits.'

Chapter Fourteen

'I couldn't believe it at first. I'd thought he'd be my husband forever.'

Jo had finally told Eve the ugly truth about the breakdown of her marriage and how she'd had to move to Boddington for a fresh start where Faith wouldn't be known as the daughter of the cheating vicar.

'And then one day he announced he was leaving me, leaving our home, even leaving the church, to start a new life with a friend of ours from the parish. Called Steven.'

Jo and Eve were on the bench at the bottom of the garden. The clouds had disappeared, the sun was out and the breeze had died down enough for them to sit outside. They were sharing a pot of tea and a tin of shortbread biscuits pinched from Maria's cupboard (Jo made a mental note to replace them) and although it was painful to talk about, Jo felt an enormous rush of relief to be getting all this stuff off her chest. Faith was nowhere to be seen, and Jo assumed she'd left while they'd been caught up with the radio interview.

'A man?' Eve said in surprise.

Jo nodded. 'Duncan stopped wanting to touch me long before we split up, but I turned a blind eye to it. He said he had a bad back and I believed him.' Tears pricked at her eyes. 'I missed all the signs. Looking back, it makes sense, but at the time...'

Eve crushed Jo to her in a fierce hug. 'You must not blame yourself. I wish you'd told me.'

'I couldn't face anyone. I was humiliated. And no one in the parish wanted anything to do with me.' Jo shuddered, recalling the look on the faces of people she had bumped into on her rare trips out of the house. 'Even the women I'd thought of as close friends melted away. Nobody trusted me, and that almost broke me.'

'You didn't deserve any of that. You hadn't done anything wrong,' Eve said grimly. 'They weren't friends at all.'

'I was guilty by association as far as the community were concerned.' Jo swiped at her tears. 'After he'd gone, the parish treasurer discovered that money had gone missing. People were convinced I must have known about it. They were more upset about the money than losing their vicar.'

'Because it hit them where it hurt the most,' Eve said darkly. 'In their pockets.'

'He didn't just steal from the church,' Jo confessed. 'He stole from me too. He took out loans in my name, and all our savings had gone. It left me bankrupt.'

'Oh my God. He's the bankrupt one – morally bankrupt, that is.' Eve growled noisily with frustration. 'I wish I'd known; I wish you'd turned to me for help.'

Jo lowered her gaze. 'I couldn't ask anyone for money. I didn't want charity.'

'You wouldn't have had to accept charity, but you would at least have had a shoulder to cry on. Plus, I'd have tracked him down and given him a piece of my mind.'

Jo smiled. 'I know you would. I'm sorry I shut you out. But I lost confidence in myself for a while, even in my ability to judge relationships. It took me ages to even apply for a job as a cleaner because I thought no one would want to trust me in their home. I had to keep going for Faith, find us somewhere to live, make a home again. If it wasn't for her, I would probably have given up and never even climbed out of bed.'

'I don't believe that,' said Eve. 'You wouldn't have been at rock bottom for long. You're too much of an optimist. And you're a natural homemaker. Whenever I stepped into your house, I always had a deep sense of peace. I felt warm and welcome.'

Tears glistened in Jo's eyes. She had been so foolish not to tell Eve everything, she already felt better for talking to her. 'Thank you. You're right, I should have told you, you are the best cheerleader I ever had.'

'I mean it,' Eve insisted. 'At first, I thought it must be something to do with you living in a vicarage and the house being holy. But then Duncan would arrive and there was a shift in the aura, as if the air became more brittle. Even your smile became brittle.'

'I always wanted to please him. He was my safe port in a storm, or so I thought.'

'You don't always need to escape from a storm,' Eve told her. 'Sometimes it's good for us to face it. Storms can be exciting – wild and unpredictable and take your breath away.'

Jo gave a snort. 'I feel as if I'm reading an Evelyn Lace novel.'

Eve laughed. 'There are similarities.'

'So what about you, how did you become a secret writer?' Jo was aware that her shoulders had relaxed from talking to her friend. It felt so good to confide in her.

'By accident.' Eve shrugged. 'It happened

during lockdown. I wasn't able to teach anyone to drive and, with all that time on my hands, I got into reading. In a massive way. Started ordering books from my local bookshop. Then I saw a competition in a magazine to write a short story. I didn't tell anyone because I thought everyone would make fun of me for trying.'

Jo laid her hand over Eve's. 'I'm your friend, I would have encouraged you, not laughed.'

'Even I thought I was an idiot for submitting my story,' Eve argued. 'Anyway, I must have been the only one who entered because I won first prize. Part of which was a Zoom meeting with a book editor to get help with my writing. I hadn't even planned on being an author at that point. She was looking for spicy romance and asked if I would write one.'

Jo's eyes were wide open. 'Just like that? This is the dream for so many people – I can't believe it's happened to you.'

'Neither can I sometimes.' Eve helped herself to a biscuit. 'Money was really tight at the time. I still wasn't working, so I thought why not?'

'What was your story about?' Jo asked, full of admiration for her friend.

'Bit embarrassing.' Eve covered her eyes with her free hand. 'About a middle-aged woman who went wild swimming off the coast of Tahiti and fell in love with a merman.'

'Why Tahiti?'

Eve hooted with laughter. 'I love the fact that you question the setting and not the love interest being a mythical creature. But I chose it because I figured not many readers of the magazine would know Tahiti well, so I didn't have to worry too much about the detail.'

'Whereas details of a merman . . . ?' Jo raised an eyebrow, amused.

'Are best left to the imagination,' Eve replied with a smirk. 'The story ended up being raunchier than I expected, and they had to edit some parts out before printing. But the upside was that my editor thought I'd enjoy writing something spicy and she was right.'

'Good for you.'

'But there was a downside to all this.' Eve's face became serious. 'I knew that Duncan wouldn't want you to be friends with the new me. And to be honest, I thought you wouldn't want to be associated with me either. Not with your role in the church community. I mean, best friends with an erotic romance author? Not a good look.'

Jo felt a wave of sadness that Eve would think that way. 'You're right about Duncan, he was such a prude. At least he used to be. But I'm so proud of you. You're flying high, doing something you love, being successful and buying a new house. Whereas I'm barely surviving, living in a rented house and trying to forget my cheating, stealing ex-husband.'

Eve shook her head. 'You've pulled through a difficult situation, you've made a new life for yourself, found work, got a roof over your head. You're doing far better than surviving, you're thriving. I used to feel a bit sorry for you. I saw you as a beautiful bird forced to live in a cage and only Duncan had the key.'

Jo considered that for a moment. 'I never really thought about it that way, but I think you might be right. Our whole life, including Faith's, revolved around Duncan's career. We couldn't even get her a kitten because of him.'

'The cage is open now, you can do anything, be anyone you want. It's never too late to change your life. I'm proof of that.'

Jo felt a surge of energy. 'You're so inspirational, Eve. I've been grateful to have this job, but I miss organising the parish diary, all the events, all the special occasions. Perhaps in a few months I'll look for something else, something to push me out of my comfort zone.'

'Good, I'm glad. If you want to be a cleaner, then great, but you could do so much more.

You were always so brilliant at organising stuff. Perhaps I can help you with a new career.'

'I'd love that,' said Jo. 'And I'd love to visit this new home of yours, I haven't even seen a picture yet.'

'You'll be my first visitor, I promise.' Eve glanced off into the distance, looking deep in thought. 'We've been a couple of plonkers, haven't we?'

'We have.' Jo held up her mug towards Eve's. 'Let's toast to being anything we want and not feeling like we should keep secrets.'

'Cheers to that,' Eve replied.

'Ta dah!' sang Faith, prancing into view down the garden towards them.

'I thought you'd gone,' Jo began. Then she let out a gasp. 'What are you wearing?'

'I found it in Maria's wardrobe when I was tidying away the pile of clothes you'd left out.'

Faith gave them a twirl to show off a low-cut leopard print camisole she'd tucked in to her black interview trousers. 'Most of her stuff gives "Nessa from *Gavin and Stacey*" vibes, but this is quite cool.'

Faith did look lovely, but at twenty-two, she would look lovely wearing a bin bag, in Jo's opinion.

'Oh my god, look at us,' Jo groaned. 'I'm

sitting in Maria's house like I own it, entertaining friends, eating her food.'

'And both of you wearing her clothes,' Eve giggled. 'Where is Maria anyway? Will I get a chance to meet her?'

'Gone to London,' said Jo, shaking her head. 'A treat for her birthday.'

'Ooh nice,' said Eve. 'Listen, why don't you two go and get changed while I do one quick job in the office.'

'Gladly,' said Jo, with relief. 'If she found out about this, I'd get the sack!'

Chapter Fifteen

The three women collected up the tea things and made their way inside.

Eve returned to the office, leaving Faith and Jo stacking cups in the sink and putting away the remains of the biscuits. She had had a brilliant idea which Jo's boss was going to love.

She took the Evelyn Lace books off the shelf and set them on the desk. Thank goodness she'd been disturbed before she'd written a message to Jo inside one of them. That would have been difficult to explain when Maria got home. And now she'd be able to sign all the books and write a special dedication in each of them for their rightful owner.

She found her special signing pen in her bag, opened the book to the first page and was about to start writing when she heard the front door open.

'Boy oh boy!' came a voice from the hallway. 'Am I glad to be home. I have had the day from

HELL, I've given up even trying to get to London. I'm exhausted.'

'Maria!' Jo squealed. 'What are you doing here?'

The sound of high heels clattering into the kitchen was followed by a gasp. Eve froze. She pressed herself behind the door out of sight, not sure what to do.

'I live here, remember.' Maria's tone was icy. 'But I might ask you the same question. Looks like there's been quite a party in my absence.'

'Oh, not at all!' Jo protested. 'Um, this is just my daughter, Faith.'

'Hey,' said Faith cheerily.

'Who appears to be wearing my clothes,' said Maria.

'So is Mum!' Faith pointed out, rather unhelpfully.

'Good grief, my dress!' exclaimed Maria. 'How dare you go rooting through my wardrobe. This is outrageous. I demand to know what is going on, Jo. I trusted you.'

'You can trust me. I promise,' Jo pleaded. 'I can explain everything.'

Eve felt for her friend. After what Jo had just told her about not being trusted by the people in Duncan's parish, Eve knew how much this accusation would hurt her.

'It had better be good,' said Maria.

'Well, what happened was, I was cleaning the oven,' Jo began.

'And you thought you'd be more comfortable wearing one of my dresses?'

'No, no,' Jo said, flustered.

'I wasn't doing any cleaning,' Faith put in. 'Just to be clear.'

Jo groaned.

Eve had to intervene. She had to rescue this situation. She quickly put on her signature red lipstick and perched her sunglasses on her head. Then, clutching the pile of books under her arm, she glided regally into the kitchen as if the whole thing was planned.

'Surprise!' she beamed at Maria. 'And Happy Birthday!'

Maria spun on her heels to see who'd walked in. Eve hid a smile; this woman really did love her leopard print.

'Who on earth are you?' Maria demanded, jamming her hands on her hips. 'And where do you think you're going with my books?'

Eve slipped her glasses down to cover her eyes and gave Maria her biggest smile. 'You mean you don't recognise me? And I think you mean *my* books.'

Maria clutched her chest and gasped. 'Oh my

goodness! Is it? No! Can it be? No. I don't believe it. Is it really you?'

Jo dashed forward and put an arm around Eve's waist. 'Maria, allow me to introduce you to Evelyn Lace.'

'Oh my god, Evelyn Lace in my house?' Maria's eyes were as big as saucers.

'It's really me.' Eve stepped forward to shake Maria's hand. 'It's an absolute pleasure to meet you, Maria. Jo has told me so much about you.'

Maria gripped Eve's hand and pumped it up and down. 'Has she? Why... when... how do you two know each other?'

'Jo and I have been best friends since forever,' Eve confirmed.

'Why did I not know that?' Maria looked amazed.

'Aunty Eve is very private,' said Faith, filming them with her phone. 'We're all sworn to secrecy.'

'That's why we had to arrange this visit while you were out,' said Jo.

'Jo wanted to do something really special for your birthday,' said Eve. 'She knew you were a big fan of my novels and had the entire collection, so she asked me to come over and sign them all.'

'This is such an honour.' Maria produced a

tissue and dabbed her eyes. 'I don't know what to say.'

Jo sent Eve a look of utter gratitude and relief.

'Thank you might be nice,' said Faith.

'Of course,' Maria stammered. 'Thank you, Jo, what a gift!

'You're very welcome,' Jo replied.

'Oh my.' Maria fanned her face. 'Can I take a selfie and send it to my husband?'

'Of course,' said Eve, thinking how much she loved meeting enthusiastic readers.

Faith offered to take some pictures. Eve held on to the books, making sure to display them properly, and Maria wrapped an arm around her. Maria selected a photograph that she liked and sent it straight to her husband with an excited voice note about Evelyn's surprise visit. Eve then insisted that they take another one with Jo in it as well.

'I'm sorry that your birthday hasn't gone as planned,' said Eve, beginning the job of writing dedications in each of the books.

Maria's nose wrinkled. 'It is disappointing, I've always wanted to see *Moulin Rouge*.'

'Me too!' said Eve and Jo together.

'Never mind.' Maria shrugged. 'Meeting you and having my books signed more than makes up for it. Oh, Nigel has replied.'

'I was cleaning the oven when Evelyn arrived, and my T-shirt was all wet,' Jo explained while Maria read her husband's message. 'I looked such a mess and Eve wanted to take a picture of me with your books too, that's why I borrowed this dress. It was wrong of me, and I apologise.'

'It's fine, I totally understand. Thank you for organising this,' said Maria, looking up from her phone. 'I really don't deserve you and I'm sorry if I jumped to conclusions. Although I'm not sure why Faith is dressed in my camisole?'

'I haven't got a good excuse,' said Faith, 'I just really like this top. I'll go and change.'

Maria shook her head. 'No need. You both look better in the clothes than me, keep them.'

'Thanks, you're a star.' Faith gave her a squeeze. Maria went pink with pleasure. 'My boyfriend has arrived to pick me up, so I'd better run, or he'll be late for his taxi shift.'

'Your boyfriend is a taxi driver?' Maria's head shot up.

Faith tilted up her chin. 'Yes, why?'

'Nigel has suggested that I get a taxi to London to join him, I know it's a long way, but do you think he'd take me?'

'I'll ask,' said Faith, thumbs already flying over her screen as she typed.

'OK.' Eve handed Maria her books back. 'All

done. Thank you for buying all my books, I appreciate it.'

'Champagne!' Maria cried. 'We should celebrate.'

Faith's ears pricked up and she put her phone away. 'I guess I could stay five more minutes for that.'

Maria produced a bottle from the fridge and poured a glass for each of them. They all toasted Maria's birthday, and Maria proposed a toast to Evelyn's next book.

'Here's to *Summer Secret Date*, may it be even more successful than your others!' Maria cried, chinking her glass against Eve's.

'Thank you,' said Eve.

'I'm so excited to read that one,' Maria confessed with a giggle. 'I've already ordered it, so I'll have it on the day it comes out. I'm going to shut myself away and read the whole thing in one go.'

Eve's heart fluttered excitedly. 'Then I've got some very good news for you. We had some proof copies printed of *Summer Secret Date*. They are highly exclusive and top secret, but—'

Maria pressed a hand to her mouth. 'Oh my goodness.'

'As it's your birthday.' Eve reached into her bag and brought out her own copy. 'This is for you.'

She held the book out to Maria, who took it from her as gently as if it was a newborn baby.

'Wow.' Her eyes brimmed with tears. 'Just... wow. Evelyn, I'm speechless. Thank you.'

'You're welcome,' said Eve. 'It was all Jo's idea.'

'But you made it happen,' said Jo, clasping Eve's hand.

'Brad says he's up for it,' Faith announced. 'So if you want to go to London, he'll take you, but you'll need to go soon. Apparently the roads are busy because there aren't any trains.'

Maria stared at the copy of the new book in her hands. 'That's really kind of him, but you know what? I think I'd rather stay here and read *Summer Secret Date*. I just don't think I can wait.'

'But the tickets?' Jo reminded her. 'Won't that be a waste?'

'No,' said Maria, 'because I'm giving them to you and Evelyn.'

'What?' Eve and Jo gasped in unison.

Maria nodded. 'Honestly, I can't think of a better way to spend my birthday than a night in with a brilliant book. I'll pay for the taxi. My way of thanking you both.'

'Really?' Jo looked as if she might cry. 'What about Nigel?'

'He'll be relieved,' said Maria. 'He didn't want to see *Moulin Rouge* anyway.'

Eve and Jo looked at each other and grinned.

'Then we accept,' said Jo. 'Gratefully.'

'Hell, yeah!' said Eve.

'This is going to be perfect,' said Jo. 'We're going to have all evening to catch up properly.'

'I have got so much to tell you,' said Eve. 'And we need to sort out a date for you to visit.' It had been a very mixed day: missing out on the trip to the printers, having her books described as pure filth, being torn to shreds on the radio. But none of that mattered. What mattered most was being here with Jo and clearing the air. She vowed never ever to let uncomfortable truths get in the way of their friendship.

'Can't wait,' said Jo. Tears ran down her face.

But Eve wasn't worried; they were happy tears – she had a few of her own trickling down her cheeks too. 'Me neither.'

She had a proposition for Jo, and she couldn't wait to share it. She was going to suggest that Jo set herself up as a virtual personal assistant, with Evelyn Lace as her first client. Eve needed an assistant, and she reckoned Jo would be brilliant at it.

'Come on guys.' Faith tapped her wrist even though she wasn't wearing a watch. 'Let's go.'

Maria walked them to the door and hugged

them both. 'You are so lucky to have each other, I'm quite envious of your friendship.'

'We are lucky,' said Jo. 'It's good to know that we've always got each other. Even if we can't be together, we message or speak every day.'

'We'll always be there for each other,' Eve agreed. 'No matter what decisions we make, or what we do with our lives, I know she'll always support me and be on my side.'

'Best friends, forever,' said Jo, blinking tears from her eyes.

Eve tucked her hand in Jo's and squeezed. 'Forever.'

About Quick Reads

"Reading is such an important building block for success"
– Jojo Moyes

Quick Reads are short books written
by bestselling authors.

Did you enjoy this Quick Read?

Tell us what you thought by
filling in our short survey.
Scan the **QR code** to go
directly to the survey or
visit: **bit.ly/QuickReads2025**

Thank you to Penguin Random House, Hachette and all our
publishing partners for their ongoing support.

Thank you to The Foyle Foundation for their support of
Quick Reads 2025.

A special thank you to Jojo Moyes for her generous donation
in 2020–2022 which helped to build the future of Quick Reads.

Quick Reads is delivered by The Reading Agency, a national
charity with a mission to empower people of all ages to read.

readingagency.org.uk   **@readingagency**   **#QuickReads**

The Reading Agency Ltd. Registered number: 3904882 (England & Wales)
Registered charity number: 1085443 (England & Wales)
Registered Office: 24 Bedford Row, London, WC1R 4EH
The Reading Agency is supported using public funding by
Arts Council England.

Supported using public funding by
**ARTS COUNCIL
ENGLAND**

Find your next Quick Read

In 2025, we have selected six
Quick Reads for you to enjoy.

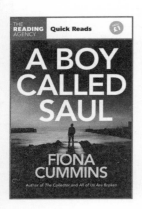

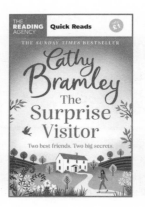

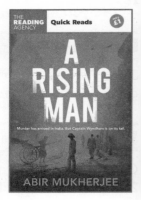

Quick Reads are available to buy in paperback or ebook and to borrow from your local library. For a complete list of titles and more information on the authors and their books visit: **readingagency.org.uk/quickreads**

Continue your reading journey with The Reading Agency:

Reading Ahead

Challenge yourself to complete six reads by taking part in **Reading Ahead** at your local library, college or workplace: **readingahead.org.uk**

Reading Groups for Everyone

Join **Reading Groups for Everyone** to find a reading group and discover new books: **readinggroups.org.uk**

World Book Night

Celebrate reading on **World Book Night** every year on 23 April: **worldbooknight.org.uk**

Summer Reading Challenge

Read with your family as part of the **Summer Reading Challenge: summerreadingchallenge.org.uk**

For more information on our work and the power of reading visit: **readingagency.org.uk**

More from Quick Reads

If you enjoyed the 2025 Quick Reads
please explore our 6 titles from 2024.

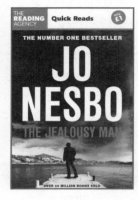

For a complete list of titles and more information
on the authors and their books visit:
readingagency.org.uk/quickreads

First published in Great Britain in 2025 by Orion Fiction,
an imprint of The Orion Publishing Group Ltd.
Carmelite House, 50 Victoria Embankment
London EC4Y 0DZ

An Hachette UK Company

The authorised representative in the EEA is Hachette Ireland,
8 Castlecourt Centre, Dublin 15, D15 XTP3,
Ireland (email: info@hbgi.ie)

1 3 5 7 9 10 8 6 4 2

Copyright © Cathy Bramley 2025

The moral right of Cathy Bramley to be identified as
the author of this work has been asserted in accordance
with the Copyright, Designs and Patents Act of 1988.

All rights reserved. No part of this publication may be
reproduced, stored in a retrieval system, or transmitted
in any form or by any means, electronic, mechanical,
photocopying, recording, or otherwise, without the
prior permission of both the copyright owner and the
above publisher of this book.

All the characters in this book are fictitious, and any resemblance
to actual persons, living or dead, is purely coincidental.

A CIP catalogue record for this book is
available from the British Library.

ISBN (Mass Market Paperback) 9781 3987 2599 7
ISBN (eBook) 9781 3987 2600 0
ISBN (Audio) 9781 3987 2701 4

Typeset at The Spartan Press Ltd,
Lymington, Hants

Printed in Great Britain by Clays Ltd,
Elcograf S.p.A.

www.orionbooks.co.uk